GEORGE O'CONNOR

HEPHAISTOS

GOD OF FIRE

First Second

New York

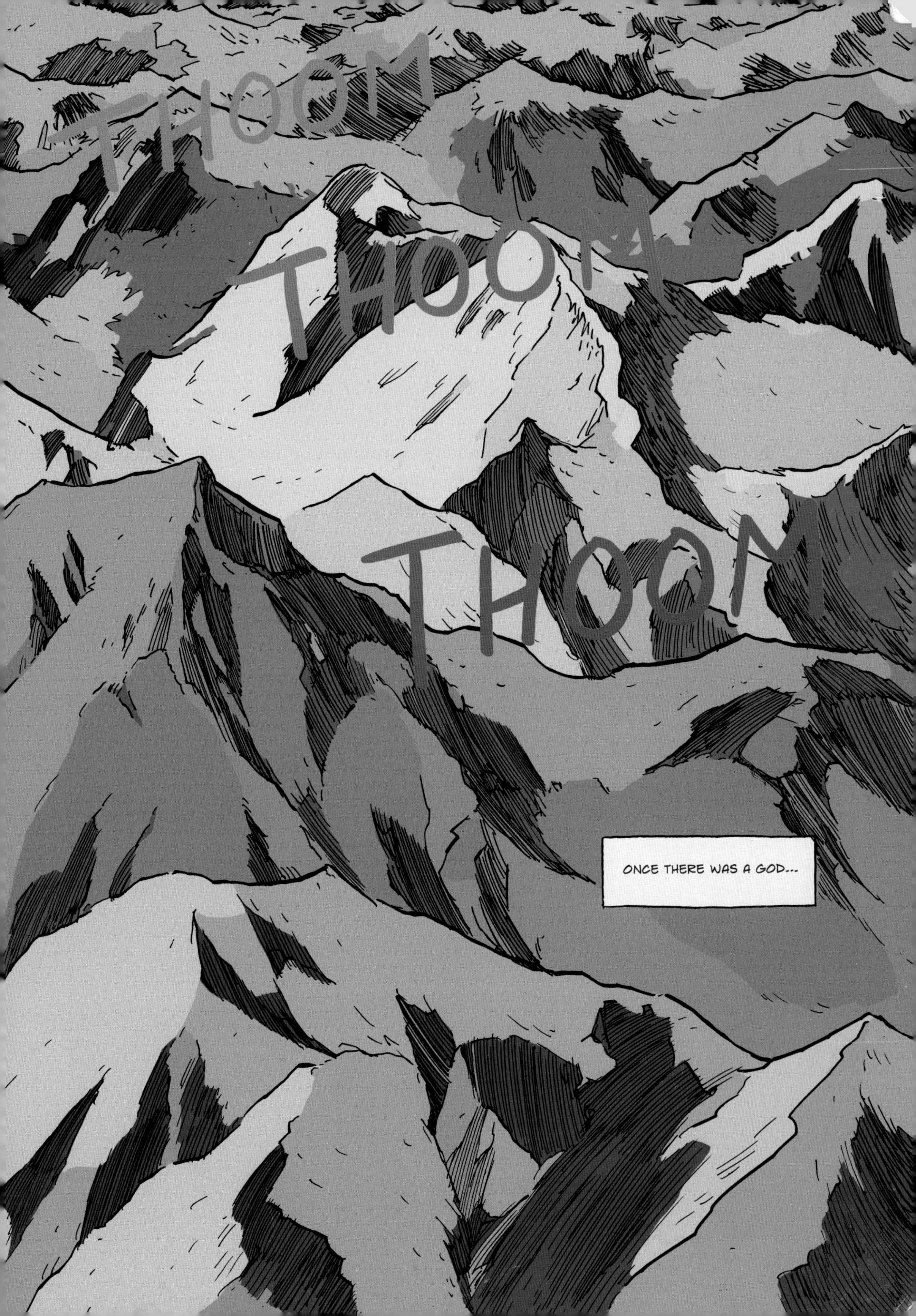
THOOM
THOOM
THOOM
ONCE THERE WAS A GOD...

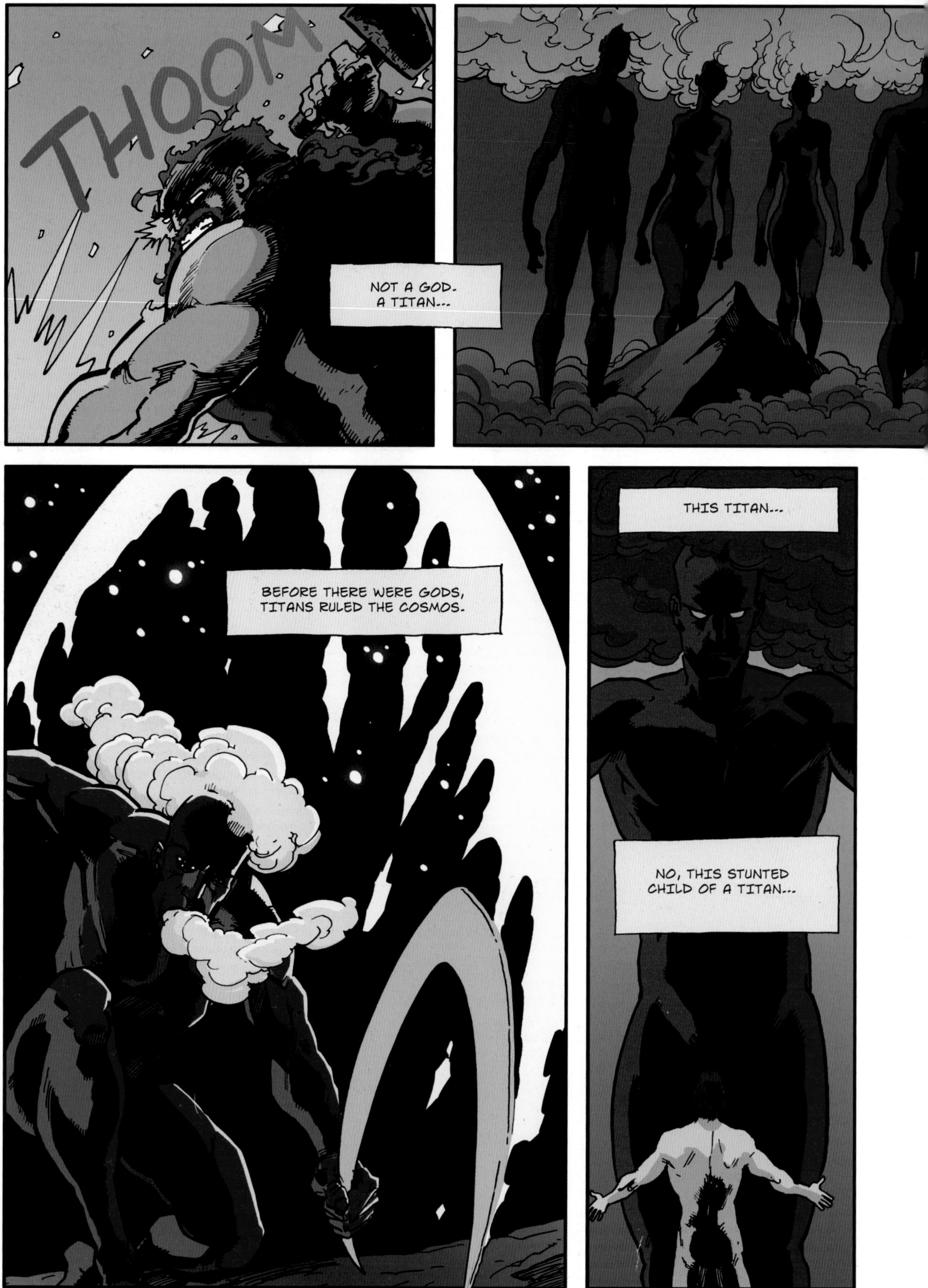
THOOM
NOT A GOD. A TITAN...
BEFORE THERE WERE GODS, TITANS RULED THE COSMOS.
THIS TITAN...
NO, THIS STUNTED CHILD OF A TITAN...

THE TITANS. GIANT, IMMORTAL, BEAUTIFUL. LORDS OF SPACE AND TIME.

THIS TITAN HAD THE GIFT OF PROPHECY.

HE KNEW THINGS THAT WERE YET TO BE.

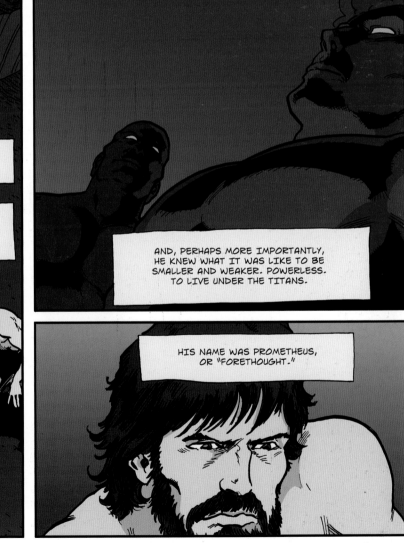

AND, PERHAPS MORE IMPORTANTLY, HE KNEW WHAT IT WAS LIKE TO BE SMALLER AND WEAKER. POWERLESS. TO LIVE UNDER THE TITANS.

HIS NAME WAS PROMETHEUS, OR "FORETHOUGHT."

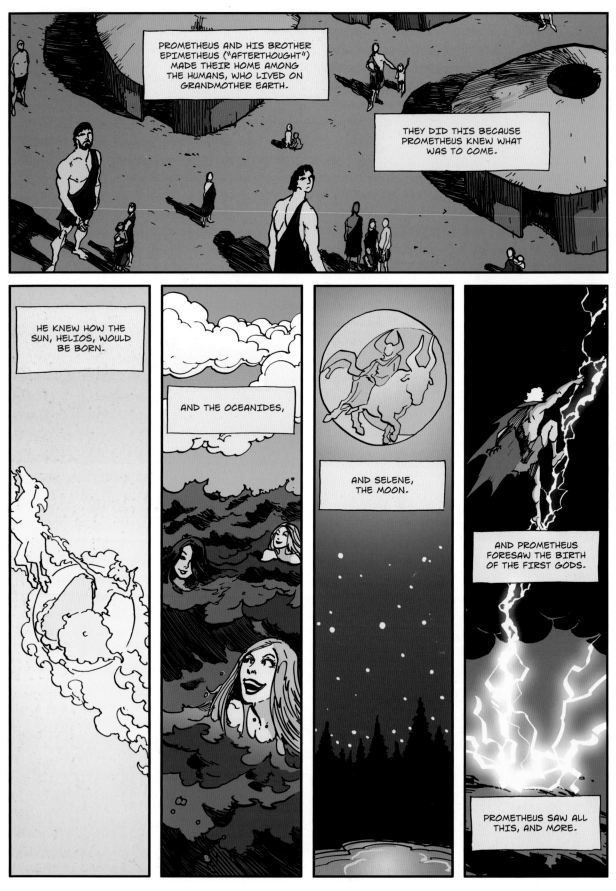

PROMETHEUS AND HIS BROTHER EPIMETHEUS ("AFTERTHOUGHT") MADE THEIR HOME AMONG THE HUMANS, WHO LIVED ON GRANDMOTHER EARTH.

THEY DID THIS BECAUSE PROMETHEUS KNEW WHAT WAS TO COME.

HE KNEW HOW THE SUN, HELIOS, WOULD BE BORN.

AND THE OCEANIDES,

AND SELENE, THE MOON.

AND PROMETHEUS FORESAW THE BIRTH OF THE FIRST GODS.

PROMETHEUS SAW ALL THIS, AND MORE.

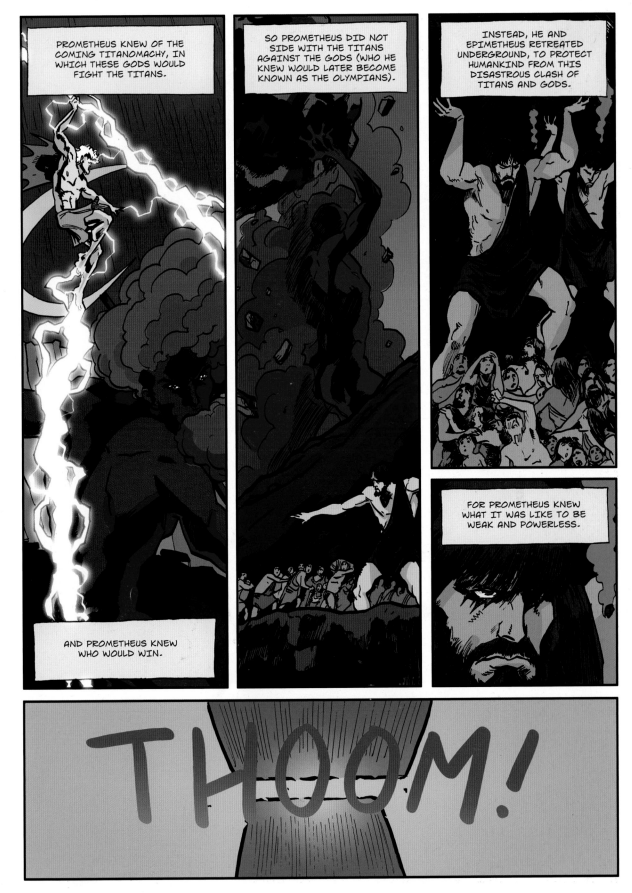

PROMETHEUS KNEW OF THE COMING TITANOMACHY, IN WHICH THESE GODS WOULD FIGHT THE TITANS.

SO PROMETHEUS DID NOT SIDE WITH THE TITANS AGAINST THE GODS (WHO HE KNEW WOULD LATER BECOME KNOWN AS THE OLYMPIANS).

INSTEAD, HE AND EPIMETHEUS RETREATED UNDERGROUND, TO PROTECT HUMANKIND FROM THIS DISASTROUS CLASH OF TITANS AND GODS.

AND PROMETHEUS KNEW WHO WOULD WIN.

FOR PROMETHEUS KNEW WHAT IT WAS LIKE TO BE WEAK AND POWERLESS.

THOOM!

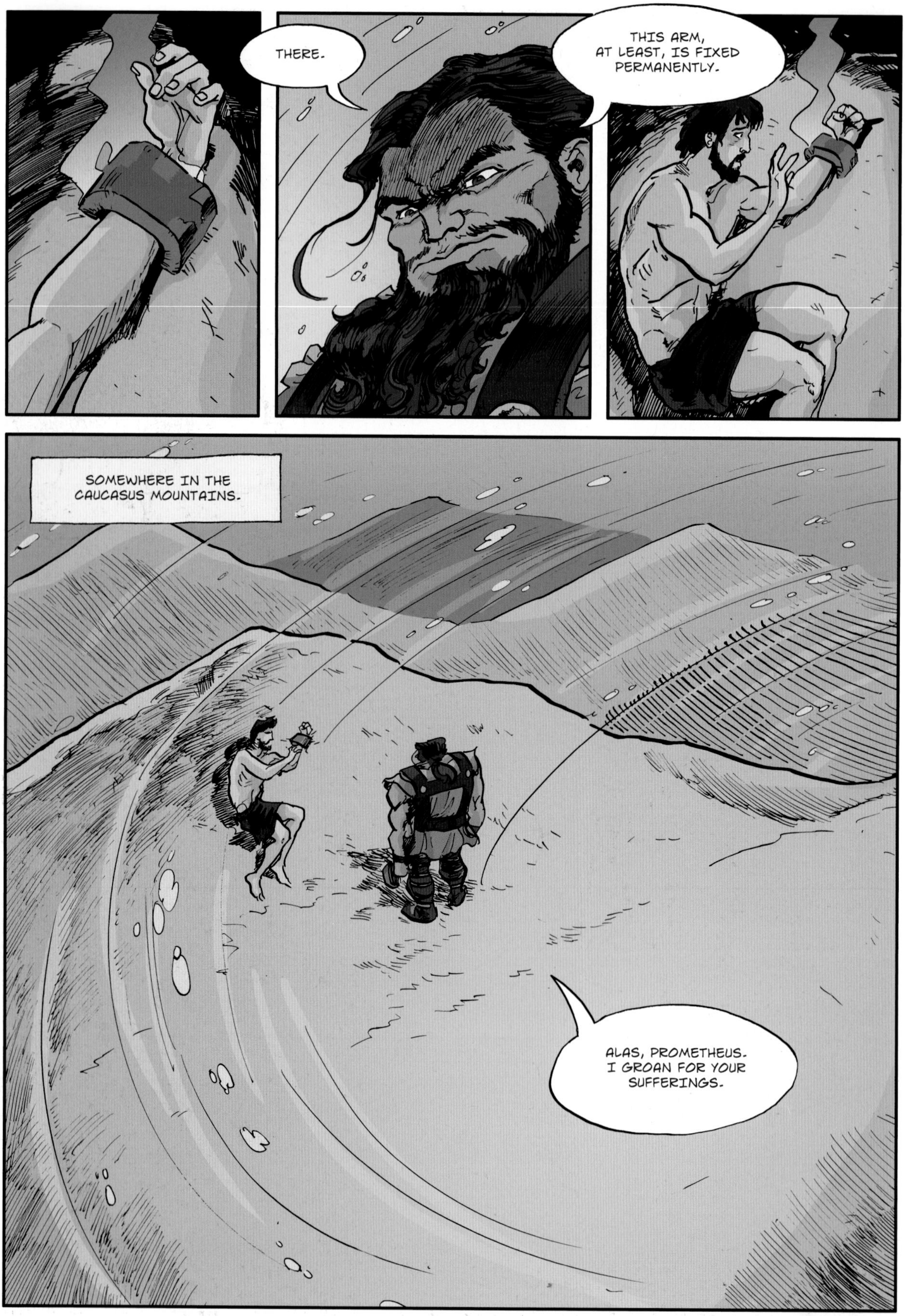
THERE.
THIS ARM, AT LEAST, IS FIXED PERMANENTLY.
SOMEWHERE IN THE CAUCASUS MOUNTAINS.
ALAS, PROMETHEUS. I GROAN FOR YOUR SUFFERINGS.

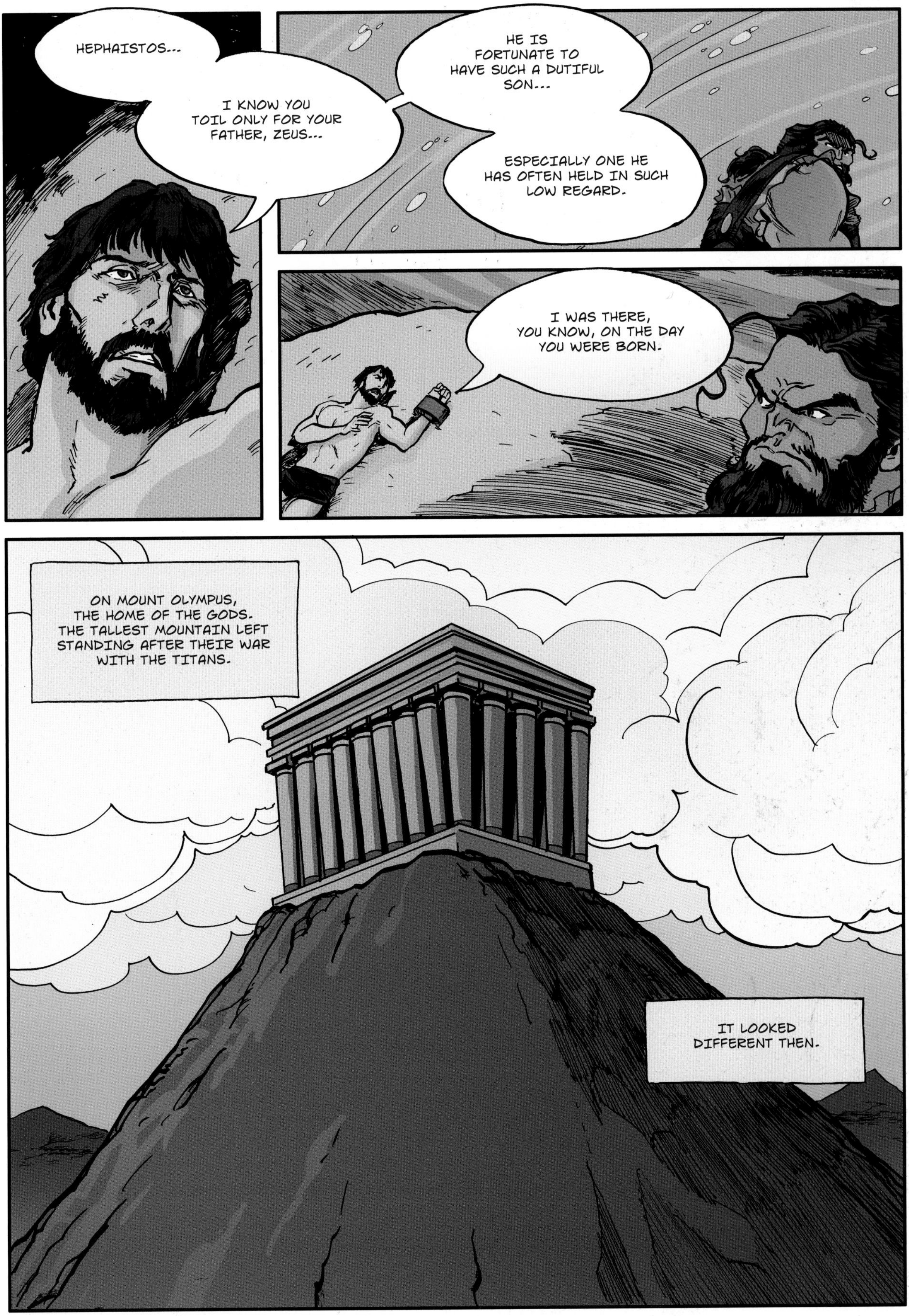
HEPHAISTOS...
I KNOW YOU TOIL ONLY FOR YOUR FATHER, ZEUS...
HE IS FORTUNATE TO HAVE SUCH A DUTIFUL SON...
ESPECIALLY ONE HE HAS OFTEN HELD IN SUCH LOW REGARD.
I WAS THERE, YOU KNOW, ON THE DAY YOU WERE BORN.
ON MOUNT OLYMPUS, THE HOME OF THE GODS. THE TALLEST MOUNTAIN LEFT STANDING AFTER THEIR WAR WITH THE TITANS.
IT LOOKED DIFFERENT THEN.

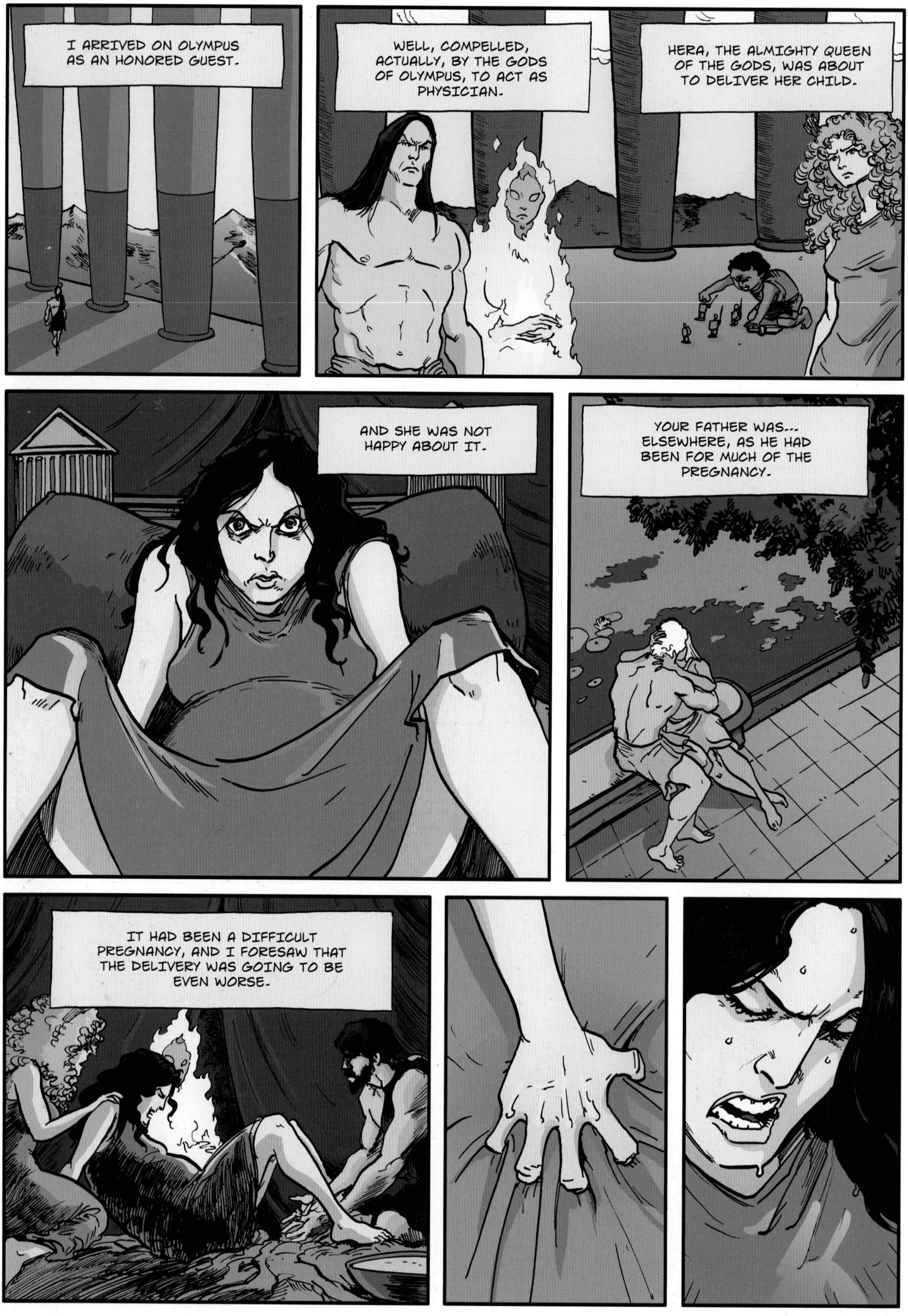
I ARRIVED ON OLYMPUS AS AN HONORED GUEST.
WELL, COMPELLED, ACTUALLY, BY THE GODS OF OLYMPUS, TO ACT AS PHYSICIAN.
HERA, THE ALMIGHTY QUEEN OF THE GODS, WAS ABOUT TO DELIVER HER CHILD.
AND SHE WAS NOT HAPPY ABOUT IT.
YOUR FATHER WAS... ELSEWHERE, AS HE HAD BEEN FOR MUCH OF THE PREGNANCY.
IT HAD BEEN A DIFFICULT PREGNANCY, AND I FORESAW THAT THE DELIVERY WAS GOING TO BE EVEN WORSE.

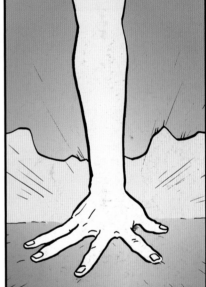

AND THEN...

9

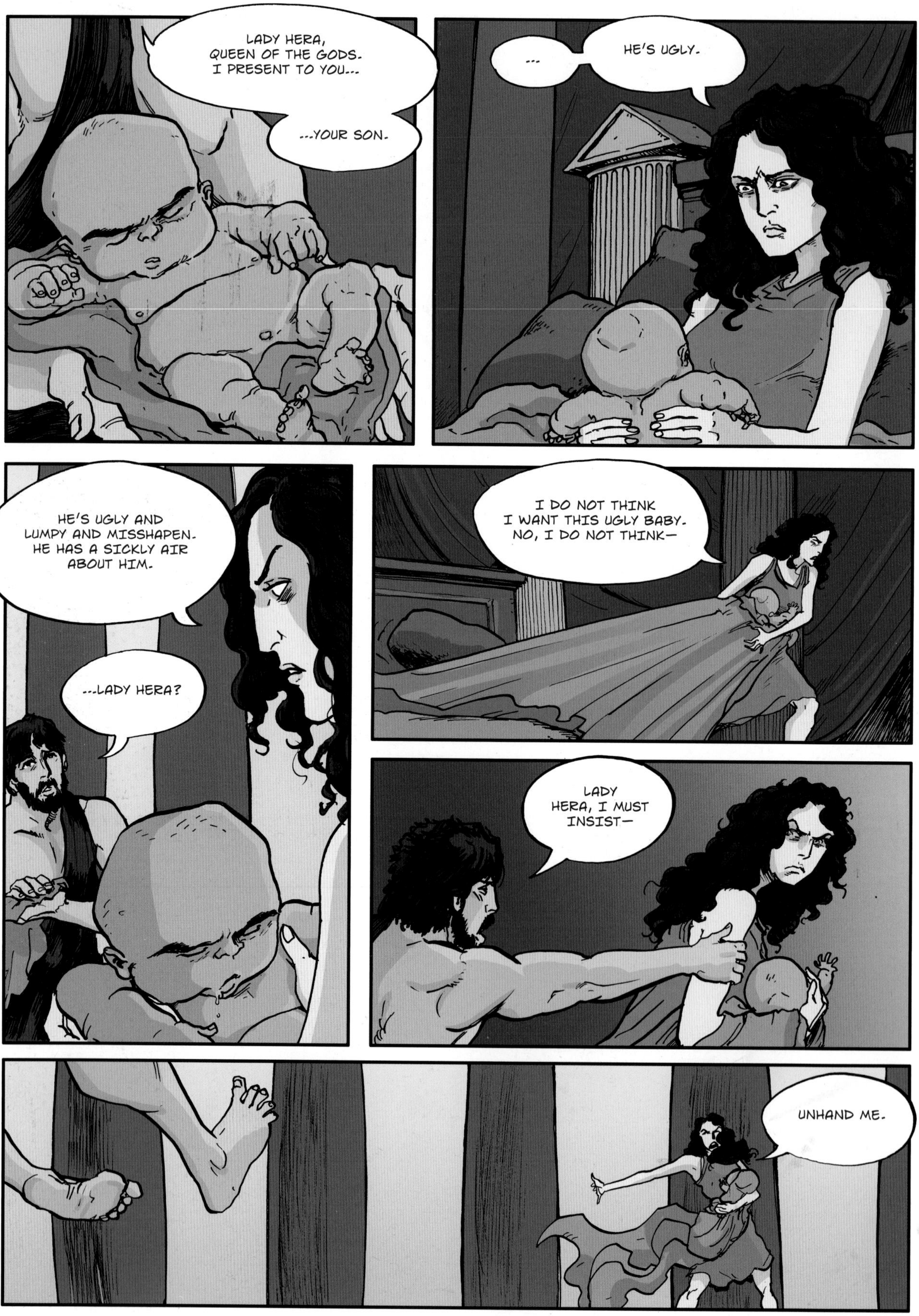
LADY HERA, QUEEN OF THE GODS. I PRESENT TO YOU...
...YOUR SON.
...
HE'S UGLY.
HE'S UGLY AND LUMPY AND MISSHAPEN. HE HAS A SICKLY AIR ABOUT HIM.
...LADY HERA?
I DO NOT THINK I WANT THIS UGLY BABY. NO, I DO NOT THINK—
LADY HERA, I MUST INSIST—
UNHAND ME.

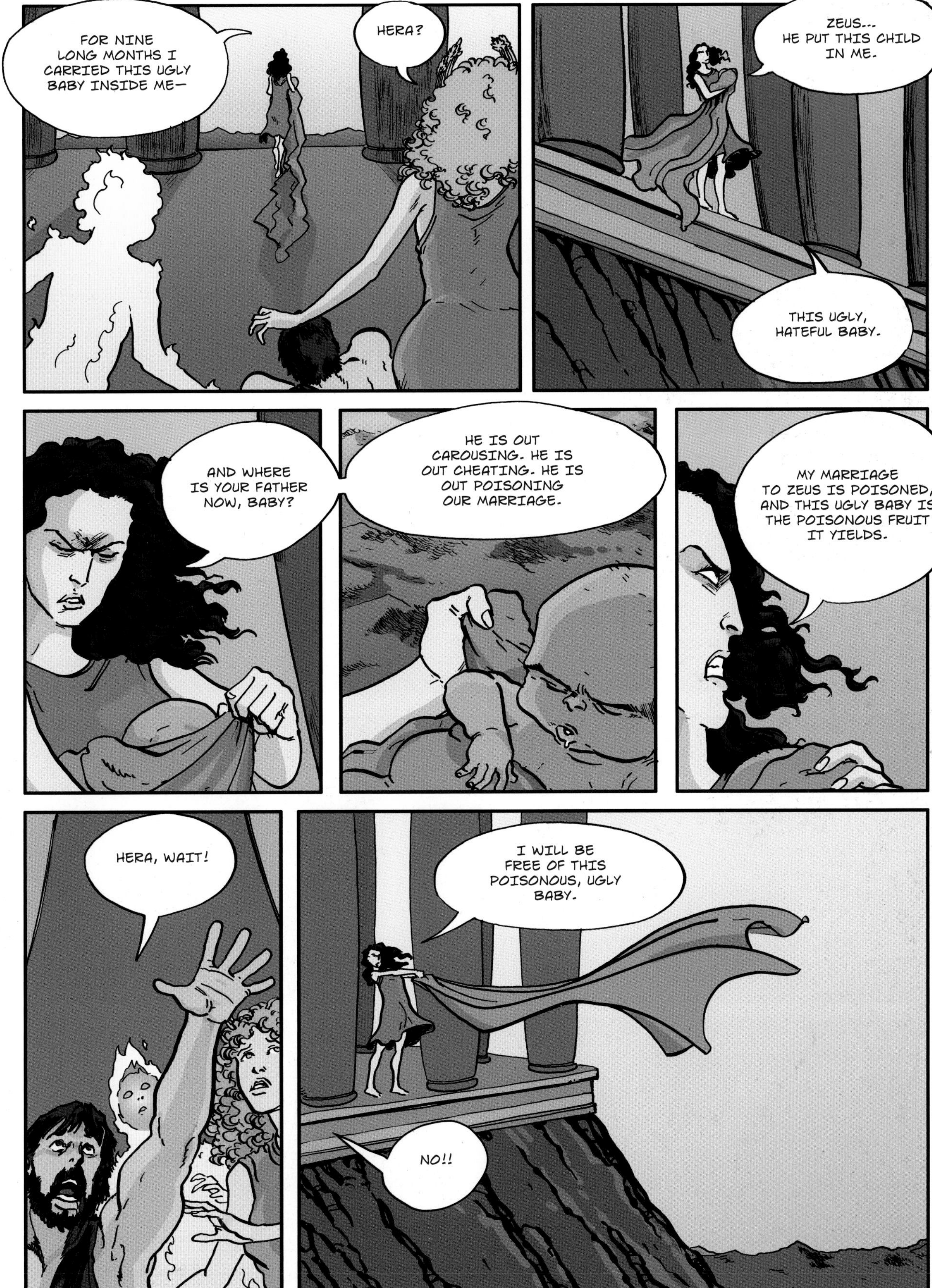
FOR NINE LONG MONTHS I CARRIED THIS UGLY BABY INSIDE ME—
HERA?
ZEUS... HE PUT THIS CHILD IN ME.
THIS UGLY, HATEFUL BABY.
AND WHERE IS YOUR FATHER NOW, BABY?
HE IS OUT CAROUSING. HE IS OUT CHEATING. HE IS OUT POISONING OUR MARRIAGE.
MY MARRIAGE TO ZEUS IS POISONED, AND THIS UGLY BABY IS THE POISONOUS FRUIT IT YIELDS.
HERA, WAIT!
I WILL BE FREE OF THIS POISONOUS, UGLY BABY.
NO!!

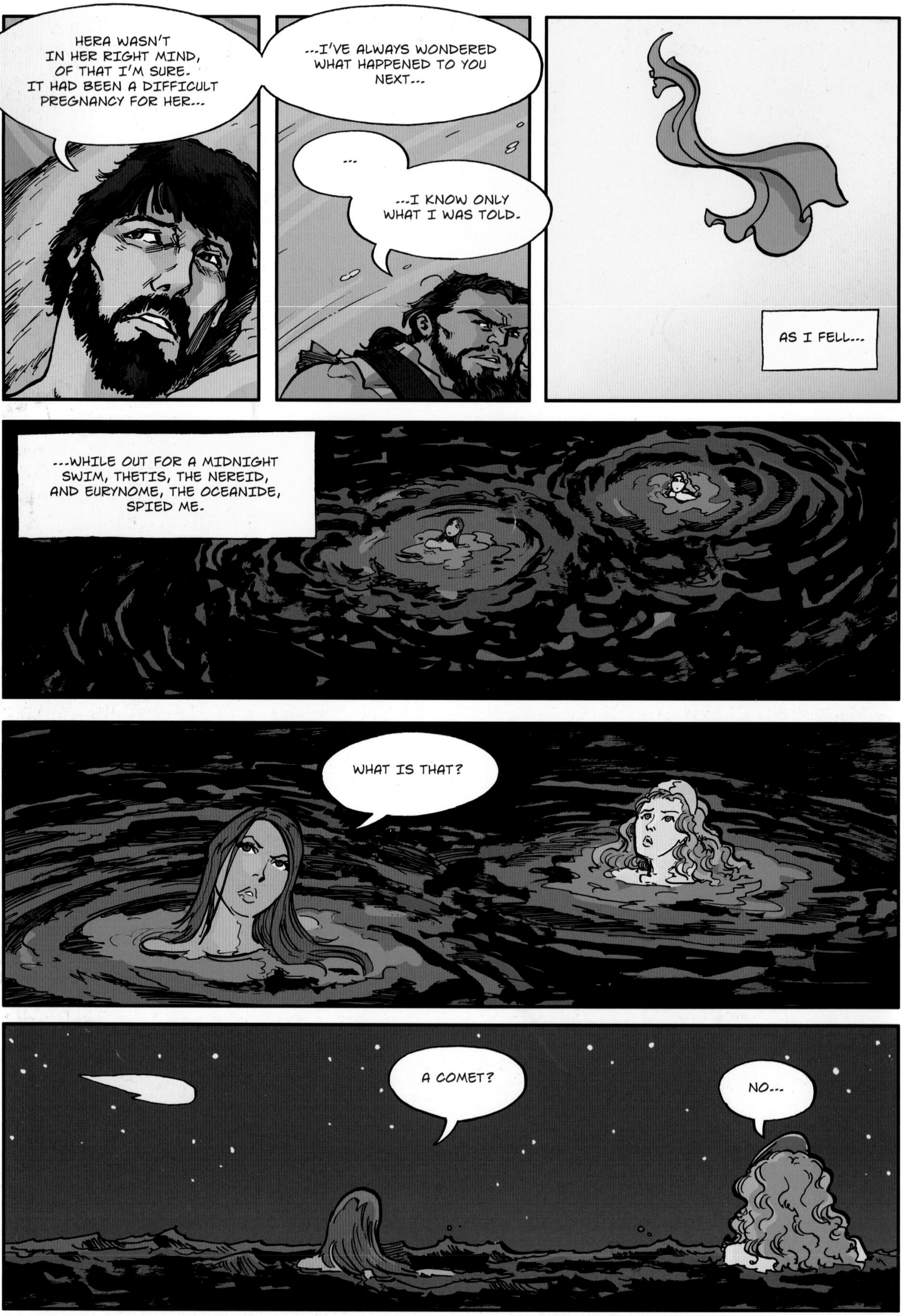
HERA WASN'T IN HER RIGHT MIND, OF THAT I'M SURE. IT HAD BEEN A DIFFICULT PREGNANCY FOR HER...
...I'VE ALWAYS WONDERED WHAT HAPPENED TO YOU NEXT...
...
...I KNOW ONLY WHAT I WAS TOLD.
AS I FELL...
...WHILE OUT FOR A MIDNIGHT SWIM, THETIS, THE NEREID, AND EURYNOME, THE OCEANIDE, SPIED ME.
WHAT IS THAT?
A COMET?
NO...

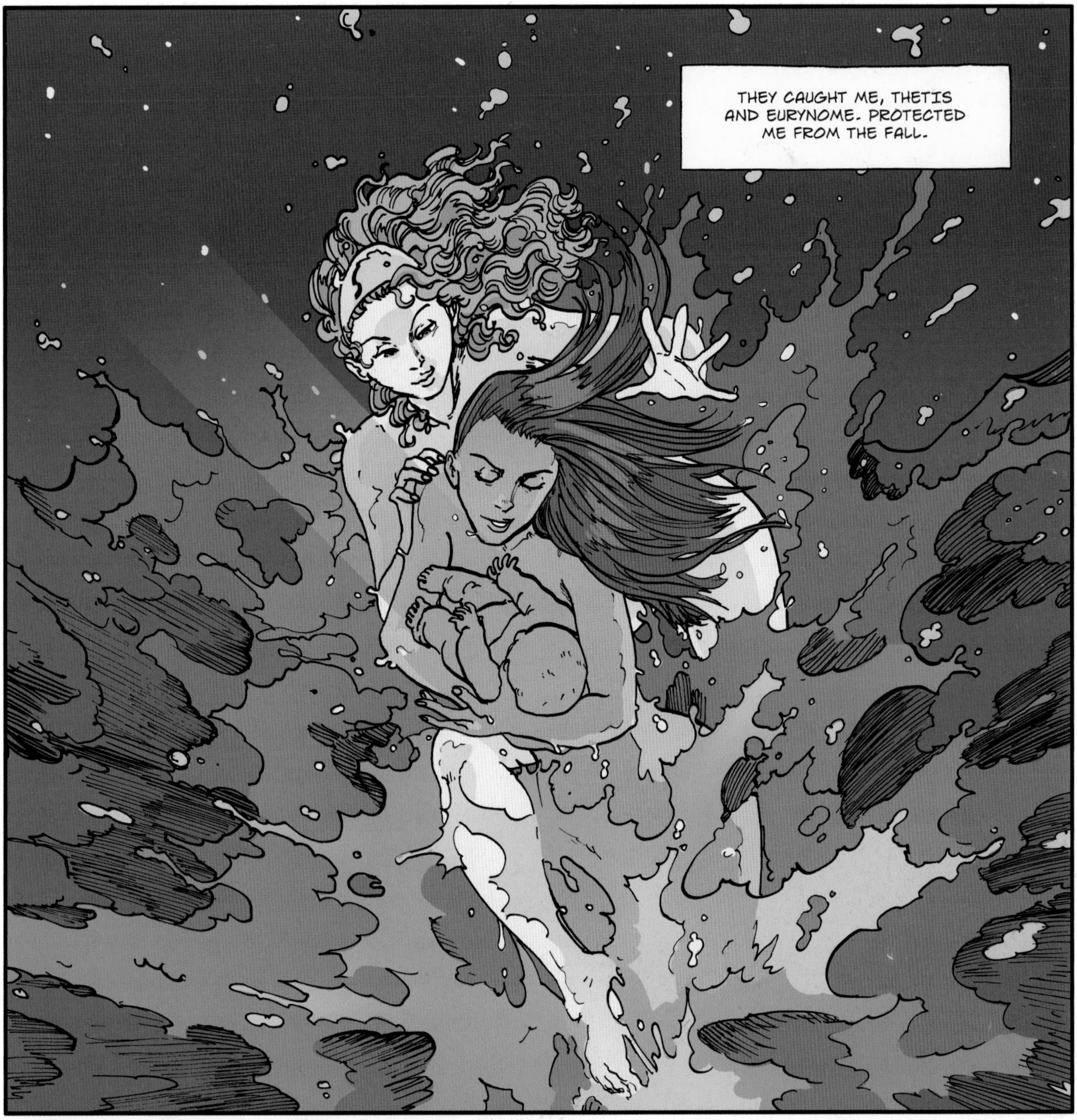
THEY CAUGHT ME, THETIS AND EURYNOME. PROTECTED ME FROM THE FALL.

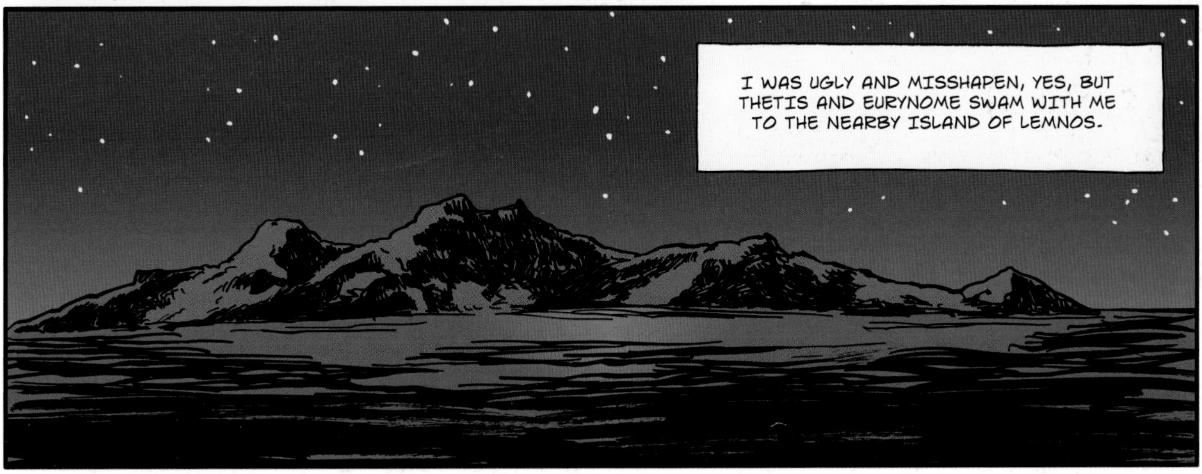
I WAS UGLY AND MISSHAPEN, YES, BUT THETIS AND EURYNOME SWAM WITH ME TO THE NEARBY ISLAND OF LEMNOS.

AND THERE WE WERE A FAMILY.

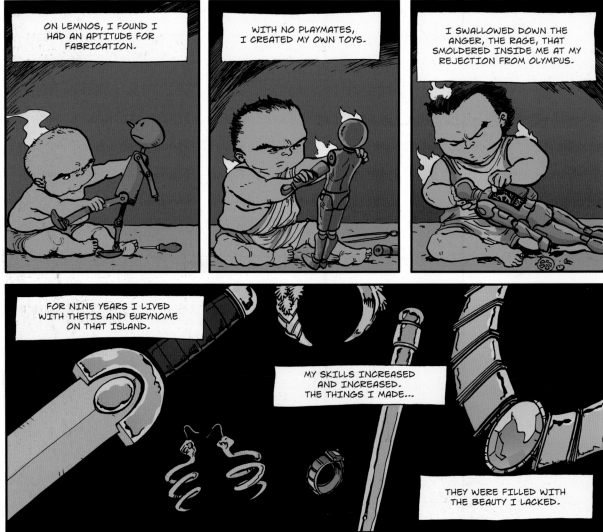

ON LEMNOS, I FOUND I HAD AN APTITUDE FOR FABRICATION.

WITH NO PLAYMATES, I CREATED MY OWN TOYS.

I SWALLOWED DOWN THE ANGER, THE RAGE, THAT SMOLDERED INSIDE ME AT MY REJECTION FROM OLYMPUS.

FOR NINE YEARS I LIVED WITH THETIS AND EURYNOME ON THAT ISLAND.

MY SKILLS INCREASED AND INCREASED. THE THINGS I MADE...

THEY WERE FILLED WITH THE BEAUTY I LACKED.

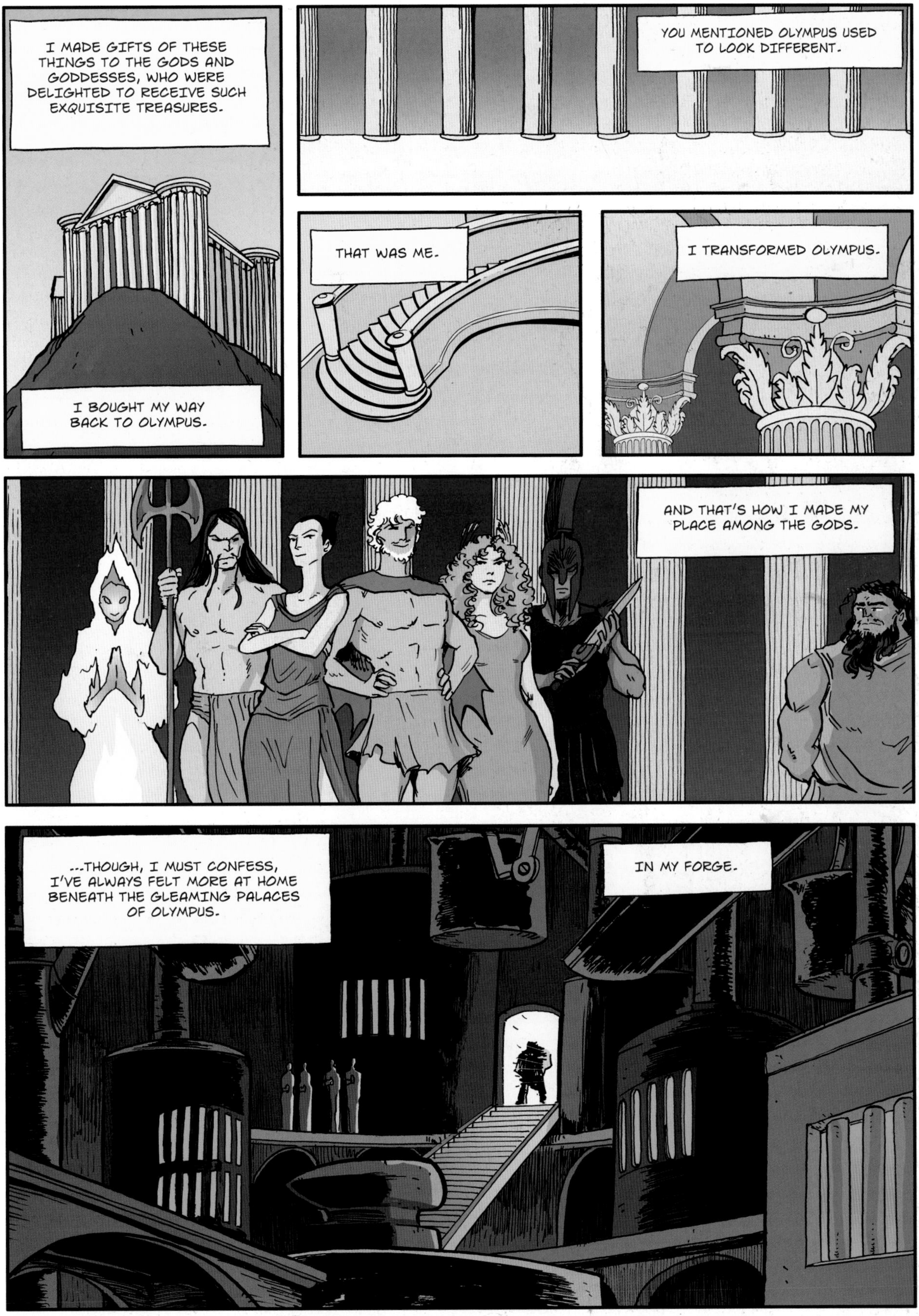
I MADE GIFTS OF THESE THINGS TO THE GODS AND GODDESSES, WHO WERE DELIGHTED TO RECEIVE SUCH EXQUISITE TREASURES.
I BOUGHT MY WAY BACK TO OLYMPUS.
YOU MENTIONED OLYMPUS USED TO LOOK DIFFERENT.
THAT WAS ME.
I TRANSFORMED OLYMPUS.
AND THAT'S HOW I MADE MY PLACE AMONG THE GODS.
...THOUGH, I MUST CONFESS, I'VE ALWAYS FELT MORE AT HOME BENEATH THE GLEAMING PALACES OF OLYMPUS.
IN MY FORGE.

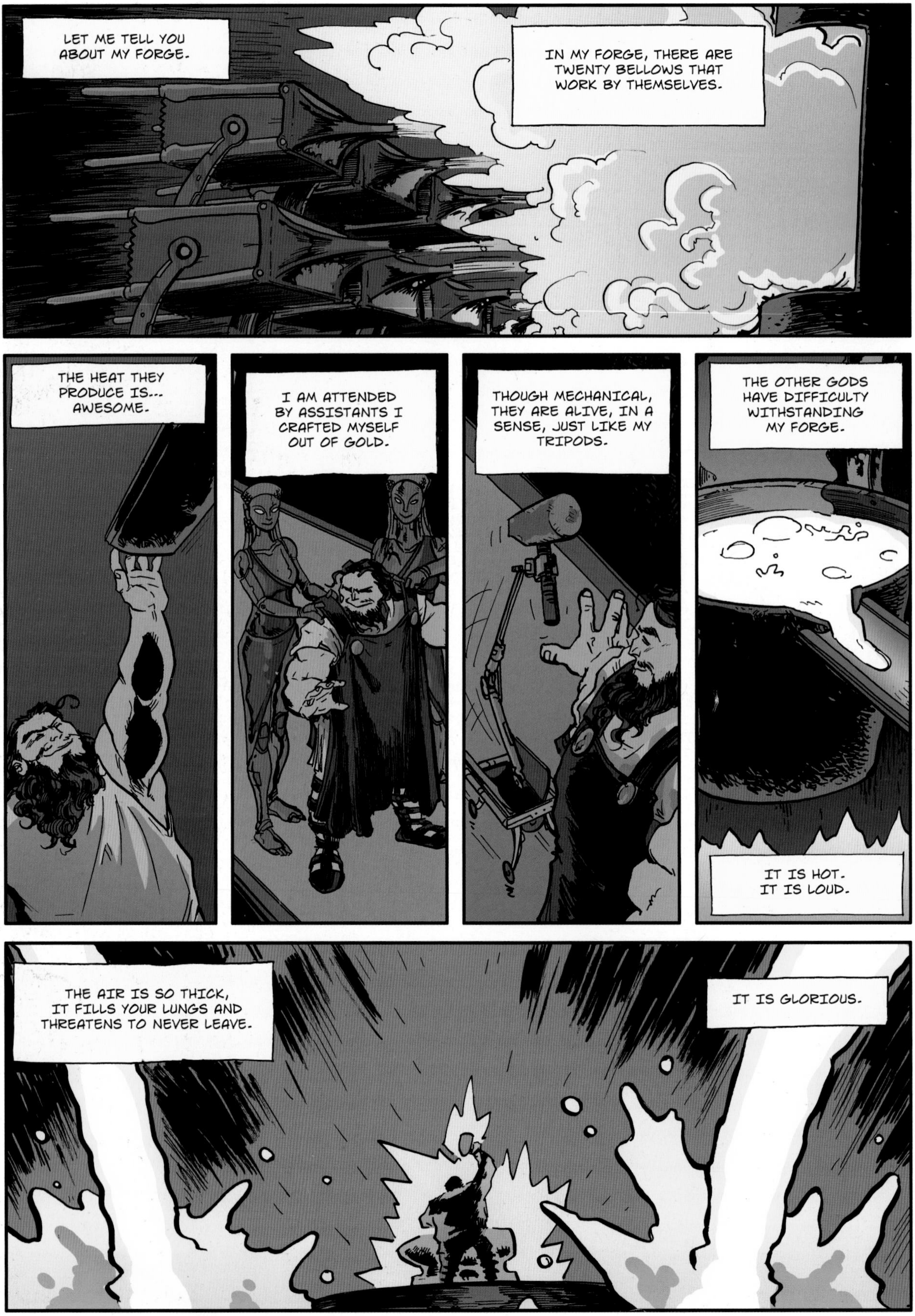
LET ME TELL YOU ABOUT MY FORGE.
IN MY FORGE, THERE ARE TWENTY BELLOWS THAT WORK BY THEMSELVES.
THE HEAT THEY PRODUCE IS... AWESOME.
I AM ATTENDED BY ASSISTANTS I CRAFTED MYSELF OUT OF GOLD.
THOUGH MECHANICAL, THEY ARE ALIVE, IN A SENSE, JUST LIKE MY TRIPODS.
THE OTHER GODS HAVE DIFFICULTY WITHSTANDING MY FORGE.
IT IS HOT. IT IS LOUD.
THE AIR IS SO THICK, IT FILLS YOUR LUNGS AND THREATENS TO NEVER LEAVE.
IT IS GLORIOUS.

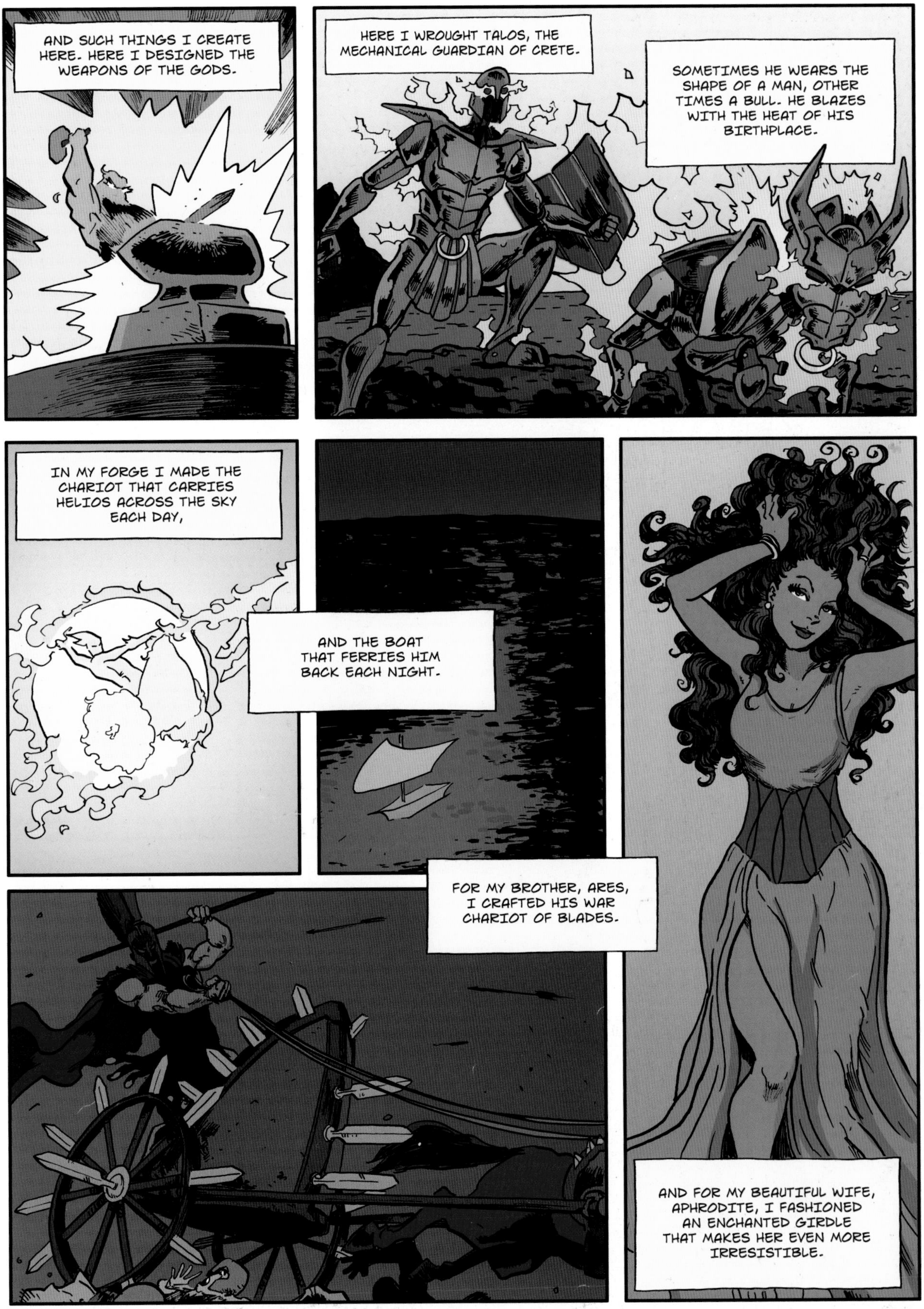
AND SUCH THINGS I CREATE HERE. HERE I DESIGNED THE WEAPONS OF THE GODS.
HERE I WROUGHT TALOS, THE MECHANICAL GUARDIAN OF CRETE.
SOMETIMES HE WEARS THE SHAPE OF A MAN, OTHER TIMES A BULL. HE BLAZES WITH THE HEAT OF HIS BIRTHPLACE.
IN MY FORGE I MADE THE CHARIOT THAT CARRIES HELIOS ACROSS THE SKY EACH DAY,
AND THE BOAT THAT FERRIES HIM BACK EACH NIGHT.
FOR MY BROTHER, ARES, I CRAFTED HIS WAR CHARIOT OF BLADES.
AND FOR MY BEAUTIFUL WIFE, APHRODITE, I FASHIONED AN ENCHANTED GIRDLE THAT MAKES HER EVEN MORE IRRESISTIBLE.

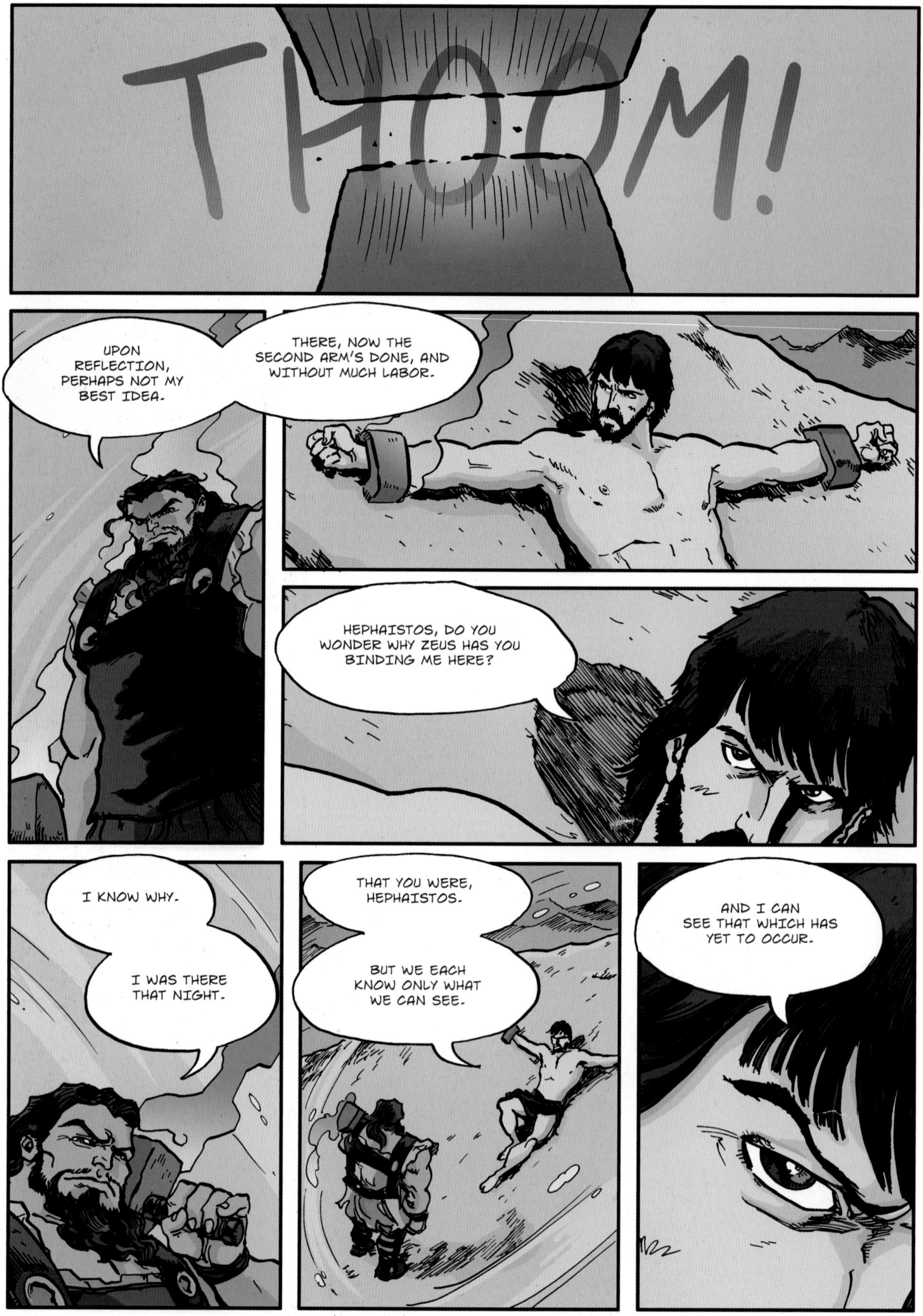
THOOM!
UPON REFLECTION, PERHAPS NOT MY BEST IDEA.
THERE, NOW THE SECOND ARM'S DONE, AND WITHOUT MUCH LABOR.
HEPHAISTOS, DO YOU WONDER WHY ZEUS HAS YOU BINDING ME HERE?
I KNOW WHY.
I WAS THERE THAT NIGHT.
THAT YOU WERE, HEPHAISTOS.
BUT WE EACH KNOW ONLY WHAT WE CAN SEE.
AND I CAN SEE THAT WHICH HAS YET TO OCCUR.

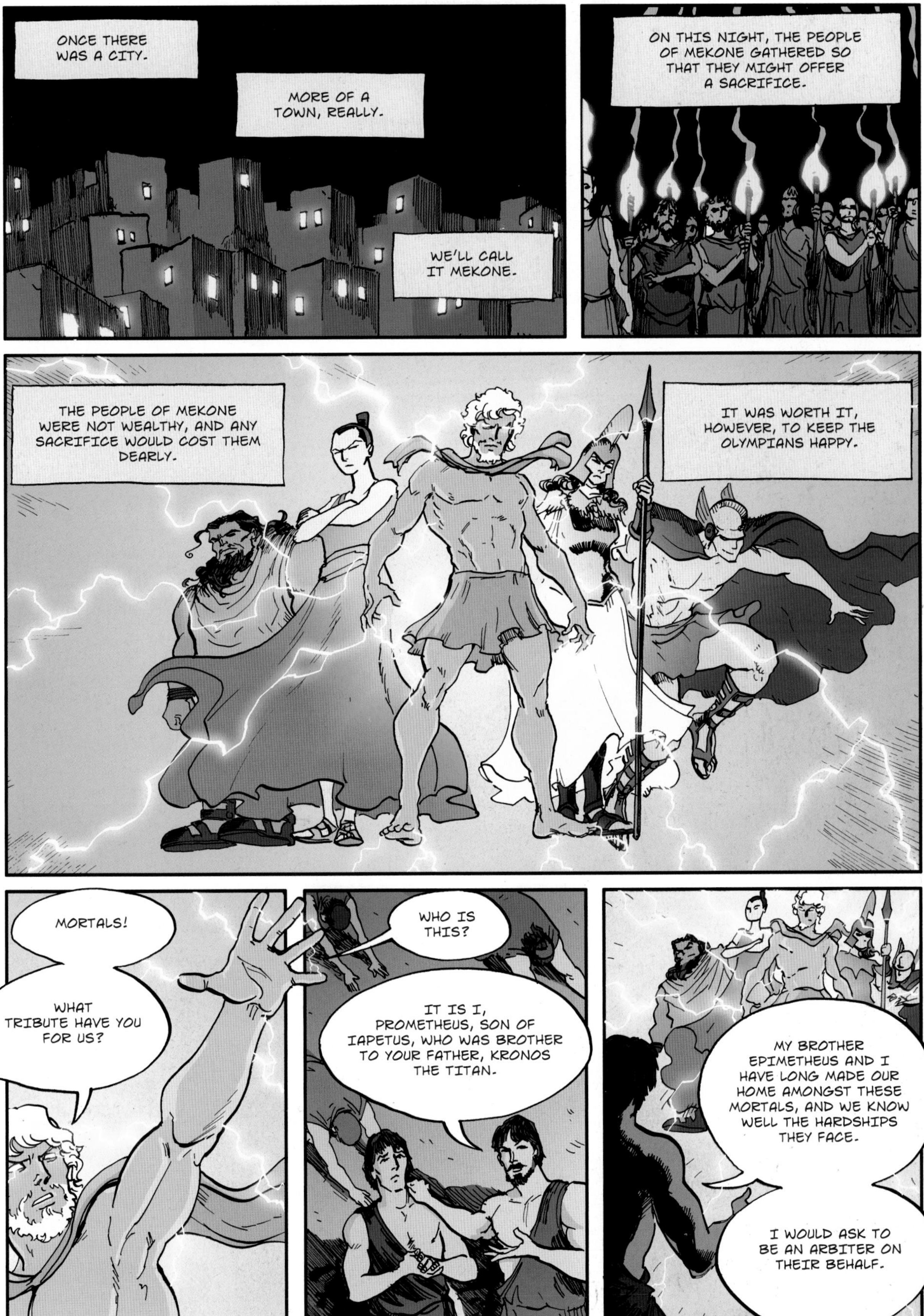
ONCE THERE WAS A CITY.
MORE OF A TOWN, REALLY.
WE'LL CALL IT MEKONE.
ON THIS NIGHT, THE PEOPLE OF MEKONE GATHERED SO THAT THEY MIGHT OFFER A SACRIFICE.
THE PEOPLE OF MEKONE WERE NOT WEALTHY, AND ANY SACRIFICE WOULD COST THEM DEARLY.
IT WAS WORTH IT, HOWEVER, TO KEEP THE OLYMPIANS HAPPY.
MORTALS!
WHAT TRIBUTE HAVE YOU FOR US?
WHO IS THIS?
IT IS I, PROMETHEUS, SON OF IAPETUS, WHO WAS BROTHER TO YOUR FATHER, KRONOS THE TITAN.
MY BROTHER EPIMETHEUS AND I HAVE LONG MADE OUR HOME AMONGST THESE MORTALS, AND WE KNOW WELL THE HARDSHIPS THEY FACE.
I WOULD ASK TO BE AN ARBITER ON THEIR BEHALF.

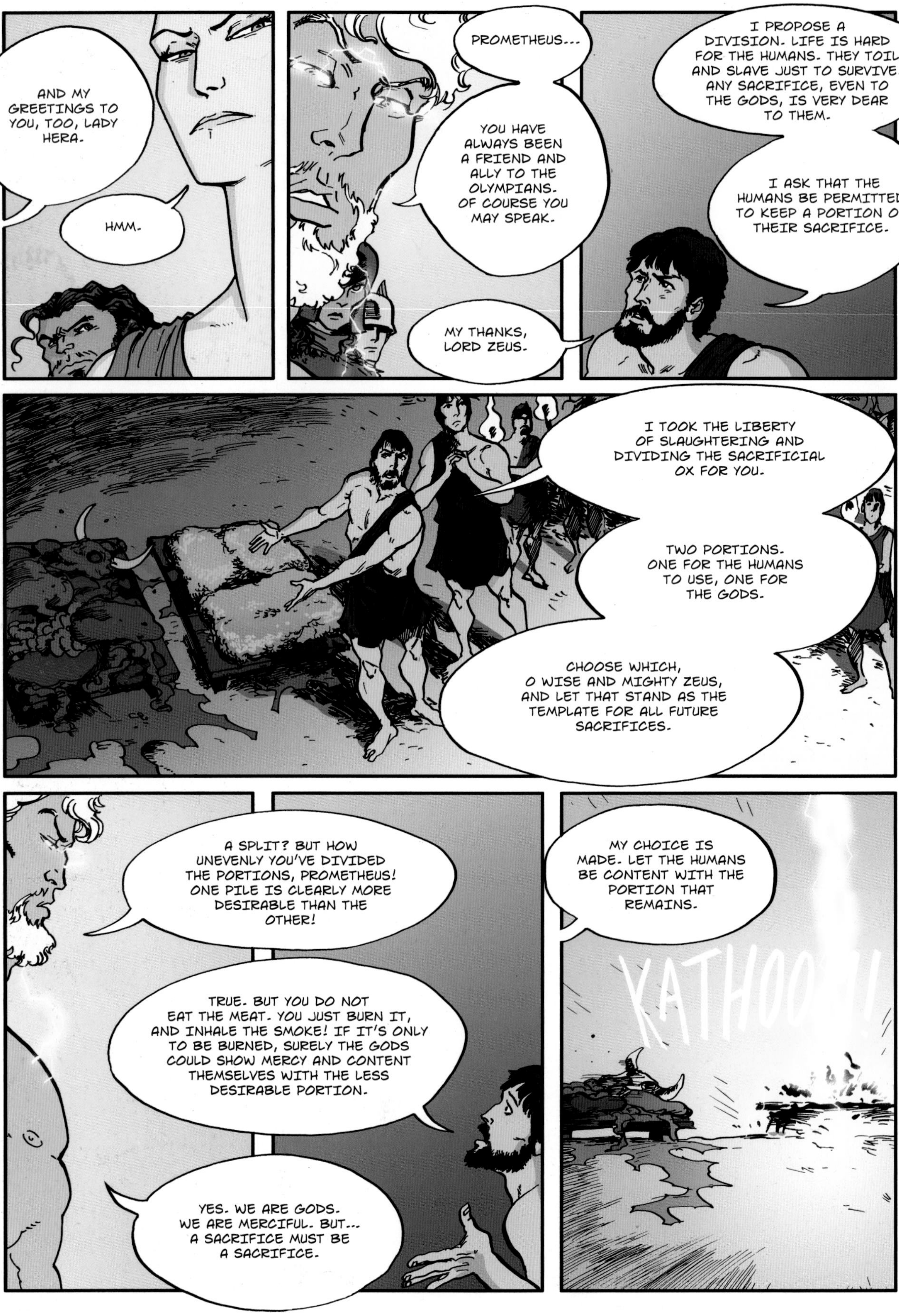
AND MY GREETINGS TO YOU, TOO, LADY HERA.
HMM.
PROMETHEUS...
YOU HAVE ALWAYS BEEN A FRIEND AND ALLY TO THE OLYMPIANS. OF COURSE YOU MAY SPEAK.
MY THANKS, LORD ZEUS.
I PROPOSE A DIVISION. LIFE IS HARD FOR THE HUMANS. THEY TOIL AND SLAVE JUST TO SURVIVE. ANY SACRIFICE, EVEN TO THE GODS, IS VERY DEAR TO THEM.
I ASK THAT THE HUMANS BE PERMITTED TO KEEP A PORTION OF THEIR SACRIFICE.
I TOOK THE LIBERTY OF SLAUGHTERING AND DIVIDING THE SACRIFICIAL OX FOR YOU.
TWO PORTIONS. ONE FOR THE HUMANS TO USE, ONE FOR THE GODS.
CHOOSE WHICH, O WISE AND MIGHTY ZEUS, AND LET THAT STAND AS THE TEMPLATE FOR ALL FUTURE SACRIFICES.
A SPLIT? BUT HOW UNEVENLY YOU'VE DIVIDED THE PORTIONS, PROMETHEUS! ONE PILE IS CLEARLY MORE DESIRABLE THAN THE OTHER!
TRUE. BUT YOU DO NOT EAT THE MEAT. YOU JUST BURN IT, AND INHALE THE SMOKE! IF IT'S ONLY TO BE BURNED, SURELY THE GODS COULD SHOW MERCY AND CONTENT THEMSELVES WITH THE LESS DESIRABLE PORTION.
YES. WE ARE GODS. WE ARE MERCIFUL. BUT... A SACRIFICE MUST BE A SACRIFICE.
MY CHOICE IS MADE. LET THE HUMANS BE CONTENT WITH THE PORTION THAT REMAINS.
KATHOOM!!

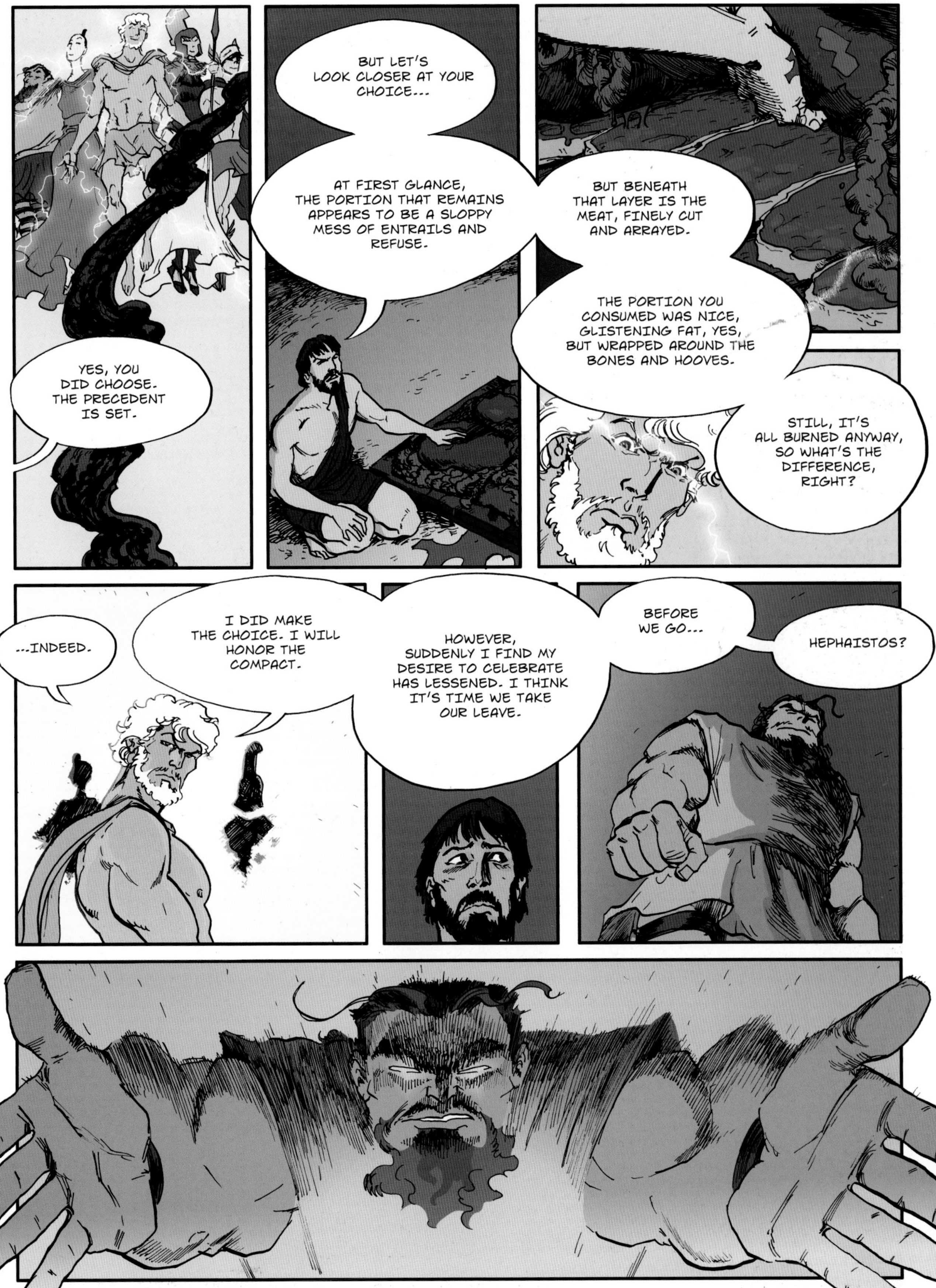
YES, YOU DID CHOOSE. THE PRECEDENT IS SET.
BUT LET'S LOOK CLOSER AT YOUR CHOICE...
AT FIRST GLANCE, THE PORTION THAT REMAINS APPEARS TO BE A SLOPPY MESS OF ENTRAILS AND REFUSE.
BUT BENEATH THAT LAYER IS THE MEAT, FINELY CUT AND ARRAYED.
THE PORTION YOU CONSUMED WAS NICE, GLISTENING FAT, YES, BUT WRAPPED AROUND THE BONES AND HOOVES.
STILL, IT'S ALL BURNED ANYWAY, SO WHAT'S THE DIFFERENCE, RIGHT?
...INDEED.
I DID MAKE THE CHOICE. I WILL HONOR THE COMPACT.
HOWEVER, SUDDENLY I FIND MY DESIRE TO CELEBRATE HAS LESSENED. I THINK IT'S TIME WE TAKE OUR LEAVE.
BEFORE WE GO...
HEPHAISTOS?

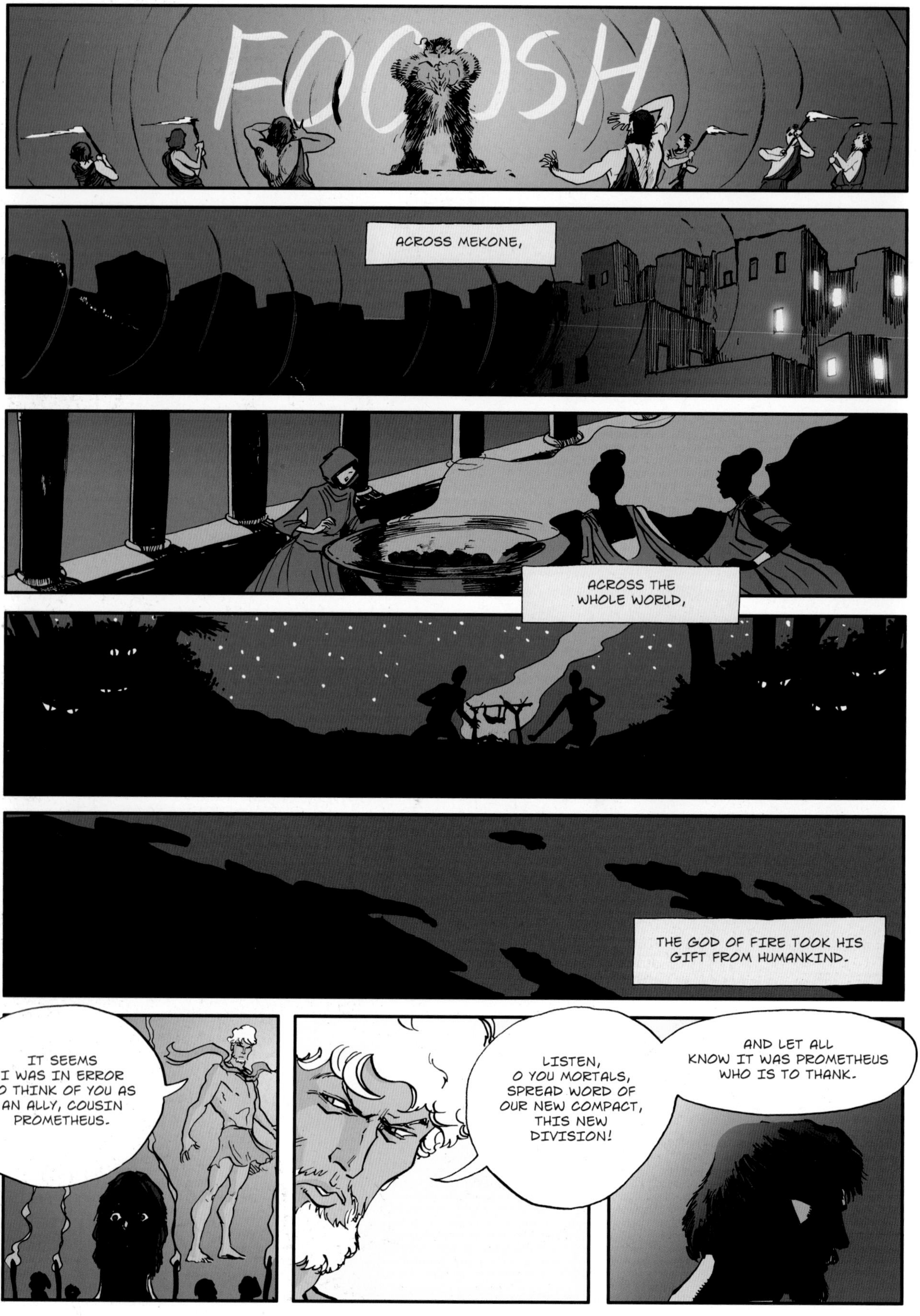
FOOOSH
ACROSS MEKONE,
ACROSS THE WHOLE WORLD,
THE GOD OF FIRE TOOK HIS GIFT FROM HUMANKIND.
IT SEEMS I WAS IN ERROR TO THINK OF YOU AS AN ALLY, COUSIN PROMETHEUS.
LISTEN, O YOU MORTALS, SPREAD WORD OF OUR NEW COMPACT, THIS NEW DIVISION!
AND LET ALL KNOW IT WAS PROMETHEUS WHO IS TO THANK.

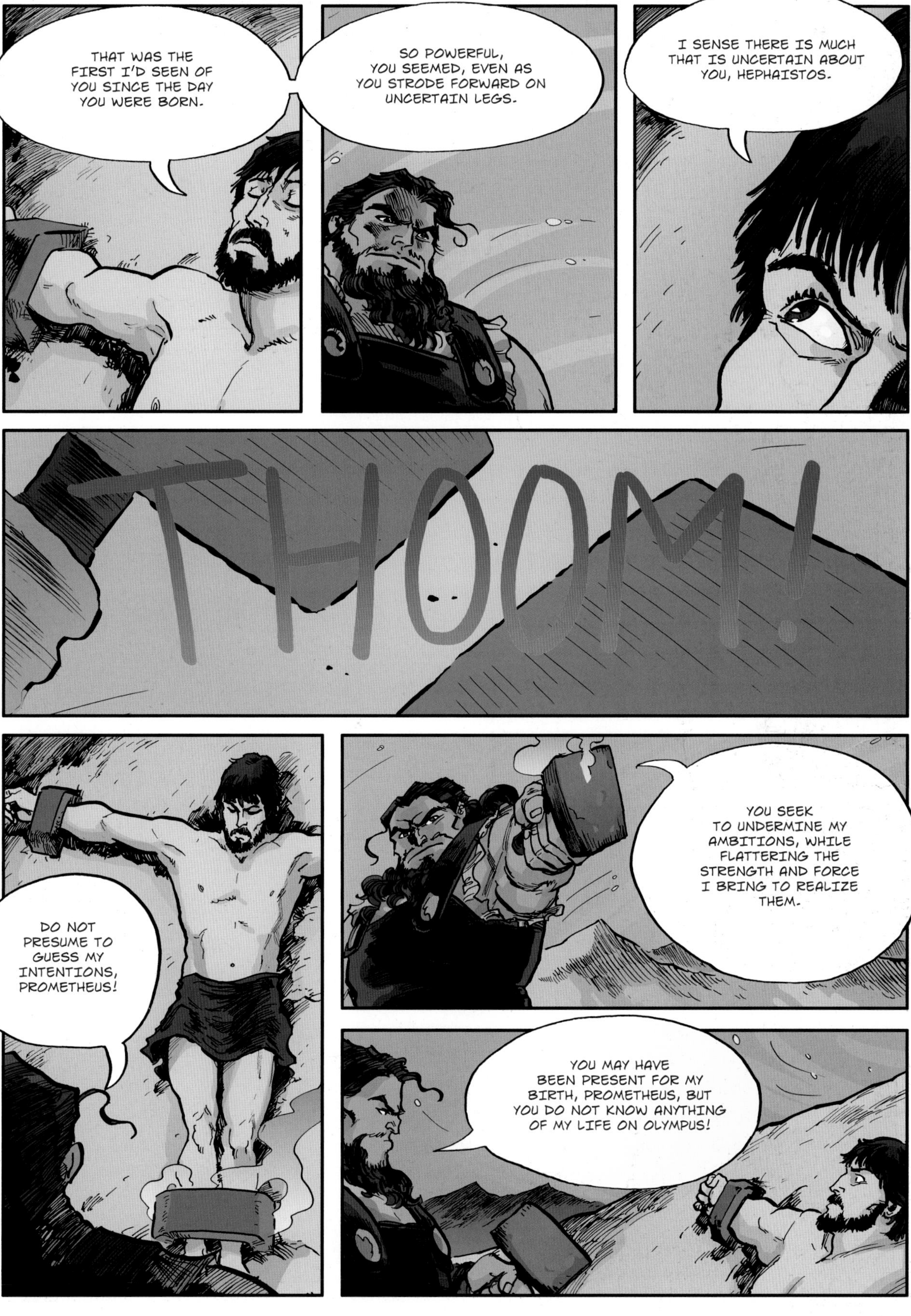
THAT WAS THE FIRST I'D SEEN OF YOU SINCE THE DAY YOU WERE BORN.
SO POWERFUL, YOU SEEMED, EVEN AS YOU STRODE FORWARD ON UNCERTAIN LEGS.
I SENSE THERE IS MUCH THAT IS UNCERTAIN ABOUT YOU, HEPHAISTOS.
THOOM!
DO NOT PRESUME TO GUESS MY INTENTIONS, PROMETHEUS!
YOU SEEK TO UNDERMINE MY AMBITIONS, WHILE FLATTERING THE STRENGTH AND FORCE I BRING TO REALIZE THEM.
YOU MAY HAVE BEEN PRESENT FOR MY BIRTH, PROMETHEUS, BUT YOU DO NOT KNOW ANYTHING OF MY LIFE ON OLYMPUS!

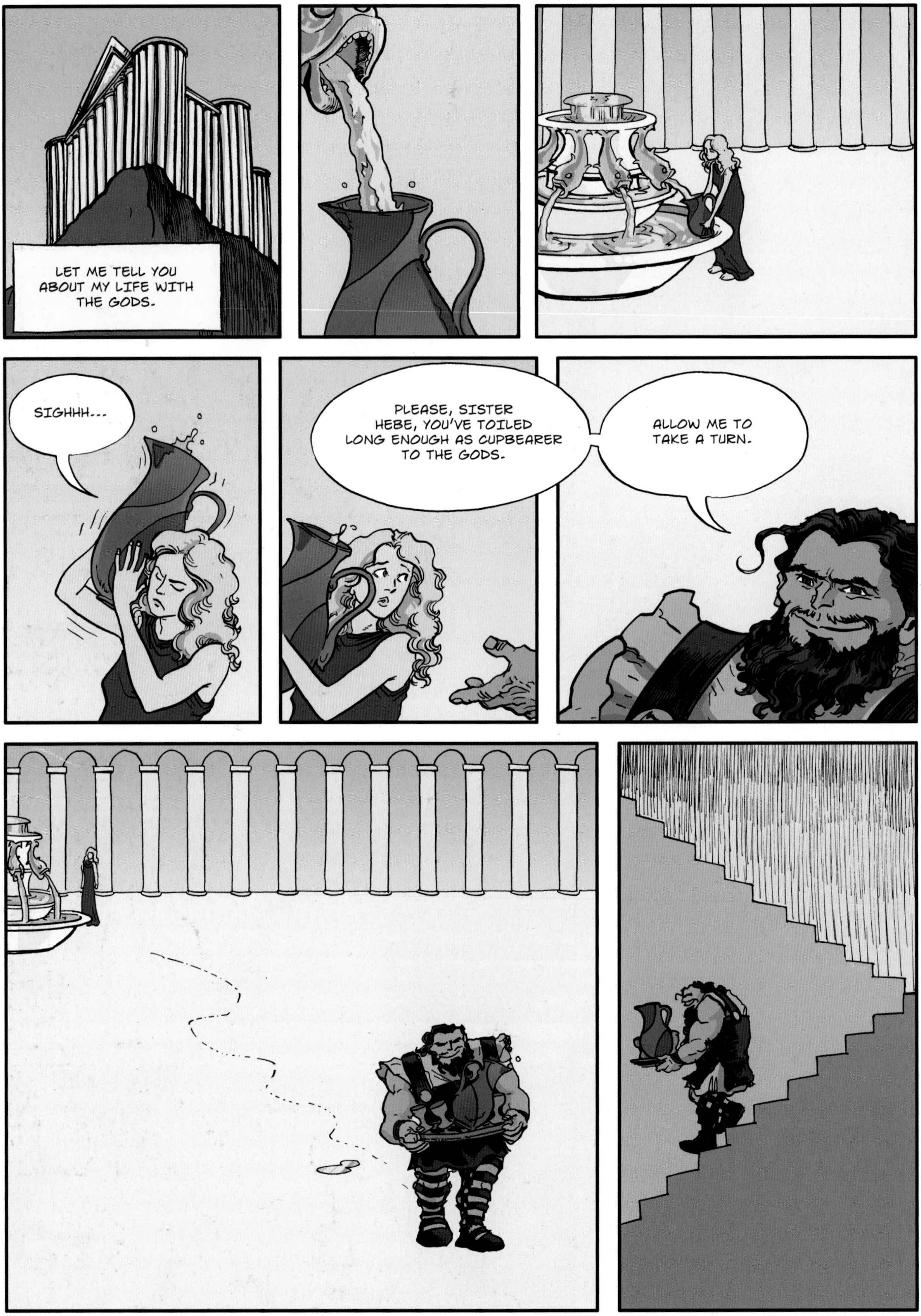
LET ME TELL YOU ABOUT MY LIFE WITH THE GODS.
SIGHHH...
PLEASE, SISTER HEBE, YOU'VE TOILED LONG ENOUGH AS CUPBEARER TO THE GODS.
ALLOW ME TO TAKE A TURN.

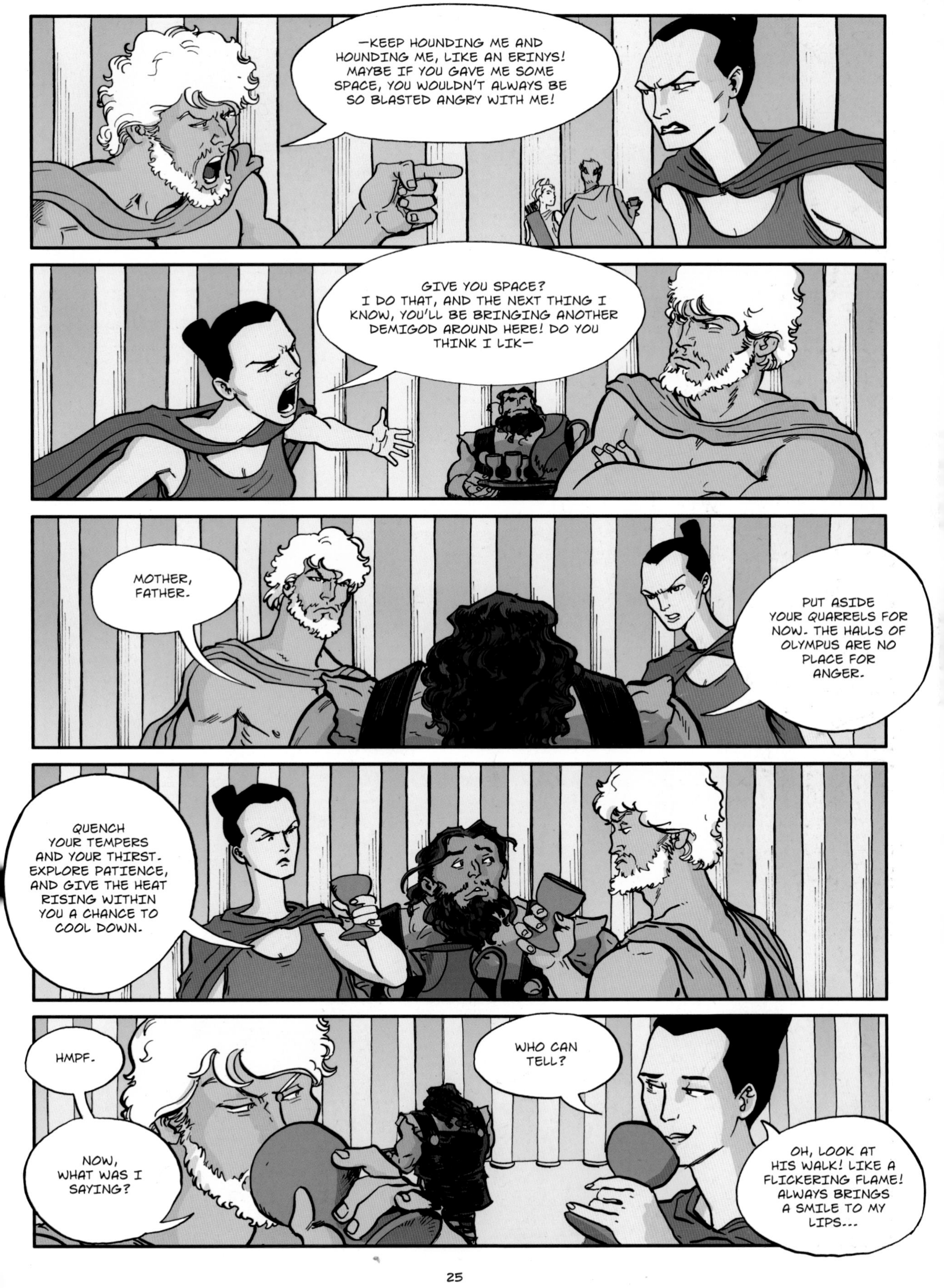
—KEEP HOUNDING ME AND HOUNDING ME, LIKE AN ERINYS! MAYBE IF YOU GAVE ME SOME SPACE, YOU WOULDN'T ALWAYS BE SO BLASTED ANGRY WITH ME!
GIVE YOU SPACE? I DO THAT, AND THE NEXT THING I KNOW, YOU'LL BE BRINGING ANOTHER DEMIGOD AROUND HERE! DO YOU THINK I LIK—
MOTHER, FATHER.
PUT ASIDE YOUR QUARRELS FOR NOW. THE HALLS OF OLYMPUS ARE NO PLACE FOR ANGER.
QUENCH YOUR TEMPERS AND YOUR THIRST. EXPLORE PATIENCE, AND GIVE THE HEAT RISING WITHIN YOU A CHANCE TO COOL DOWN.
HMPF.
NOW, WHAT WAS I SAYING?
WHO CAN TELL?
OH, LOOK AT HIS WALK! LIKE A FLICKERING FLAME! ALWAYS BRINGS A SMILE TO MY LIPS...

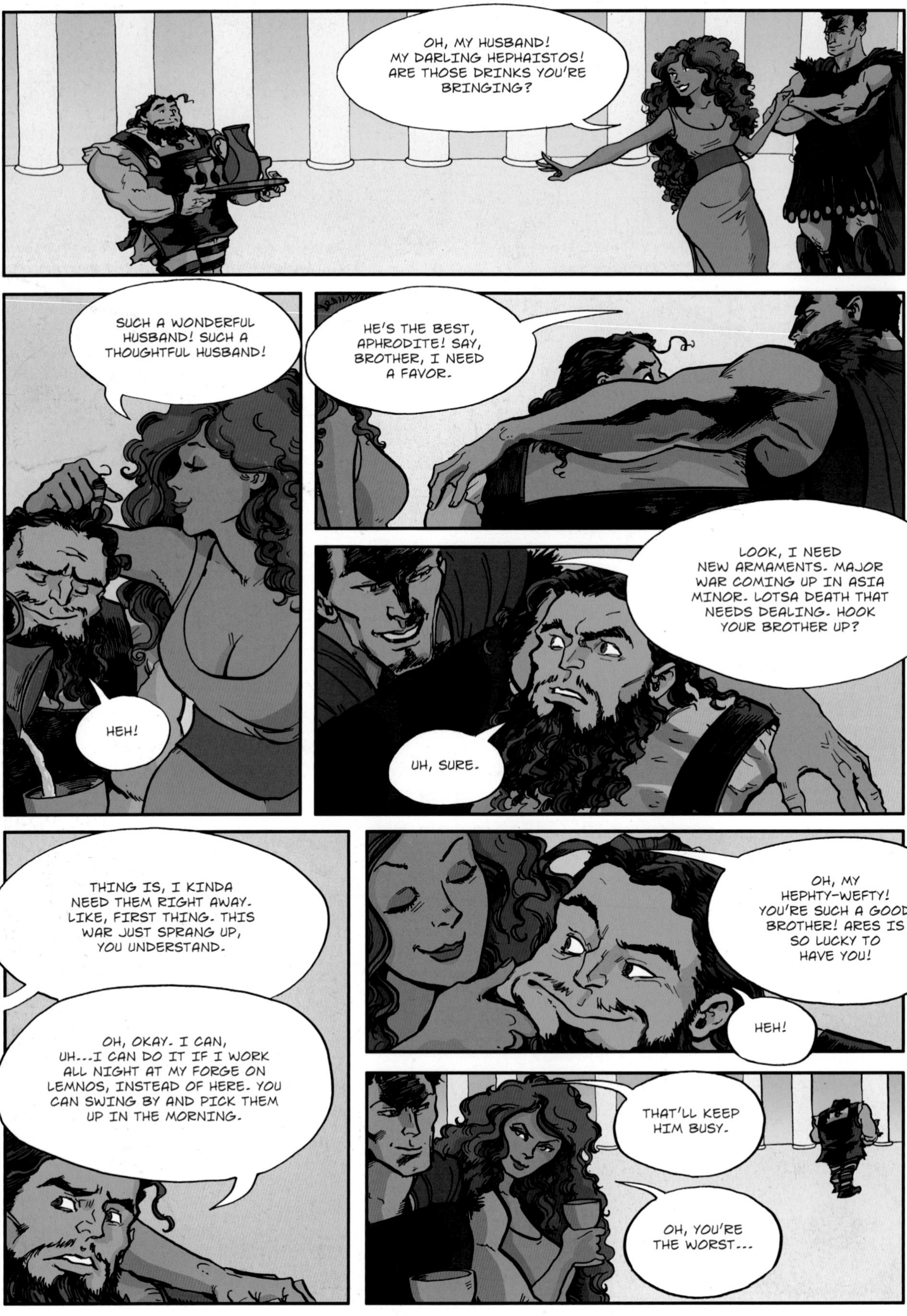
OH, MY HUSBAND! MY DARLING HEPHAISTOS! ARE THOSE DRINKS YOU'RE BRINGING?
SUCH A WONDERFUL HUSBAND! SUCH A THOUGHTFUL HUSBAND!
HEH!
HE'S THE BEST, APHRODITE! SAY, BROTHER, I NEED A FAVOR.
LOOK, I NEED NEW ARMAMENTS. MAJOR WAR COMING UP IN ASIA MINOR. LOTSA DEATH THAT NEEDS DEALING. HOOK YOUR BROTHER UP?
UH, SURE.
THING IS, I KINDA NEED THEM RIGHT AWAY. LIKE, FIRST THING. THIS WAR JUST SPRANG UP, YOU UNDERSTAND.
OH, OKAY. I CAN, UH...I CAN DO IT IF I WORK ALL NIGHT AT MY FORGE ON LEMNOS, INSTEAD OF HERE. YOU CAN SWING BY AND PICK THEM UP IN THE MORNING.
OH, MY HEPHTY-WEFTY! YOU'RE SUCH A GOOD BROTHER! ARES IS SO LUCKY TO HAVE YOU!
HEH!
THAT'LL KEEP HIM BUSY.
OH, YOU'RE THE WORST...

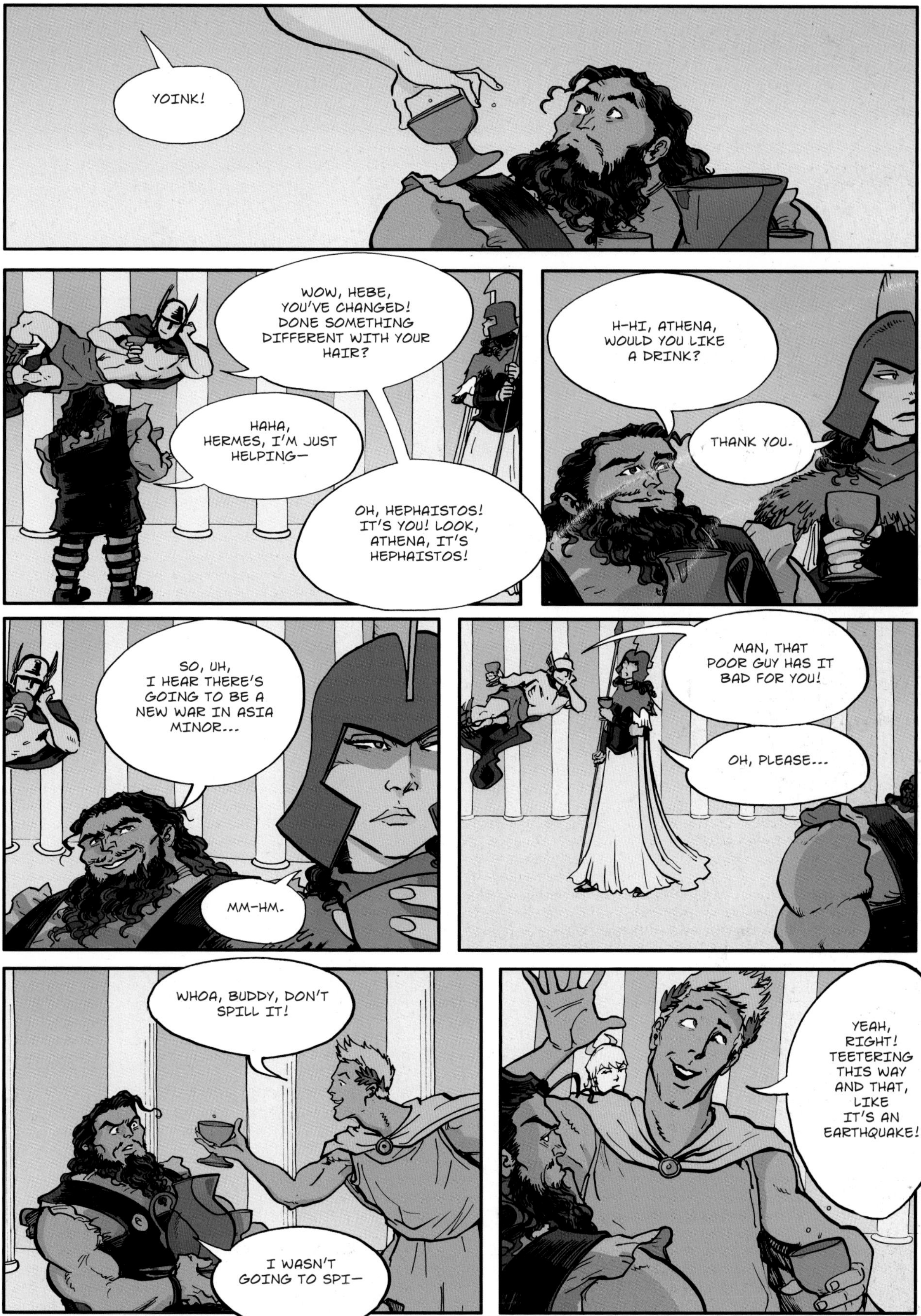

YOINK!
WOW, HEBE, YOU'VE CHANGED! DONE SOMETHING DIFFERENT WITH YOUR HAIR?
HAHA, HERMES, I'M JUST HELPING—
OH, HEPHAISTOS! IT'S YOU! LOOK, ATHENA, IT'S HEPHAISTOS!
H-HI, ATHENA, WOULD YOU LIKE A DRINK?
THANK YOU.
SO, UH, I HEAR THERE'S GOING TO BE A NEW WAR IN ASIA MINOR...
MM-HM.
MAN, THAT POOR GUY HAS IT BAD FOR YOU!
OH, PLEASE...
WHOA, BUDDY, DON'T SPILL IT!
I WASN'T GOING TO SPI—
YEAH, RIGHT! TEETERING THIS WAY AND THAT, LIKE IT'S AN EARTHQUAKE!

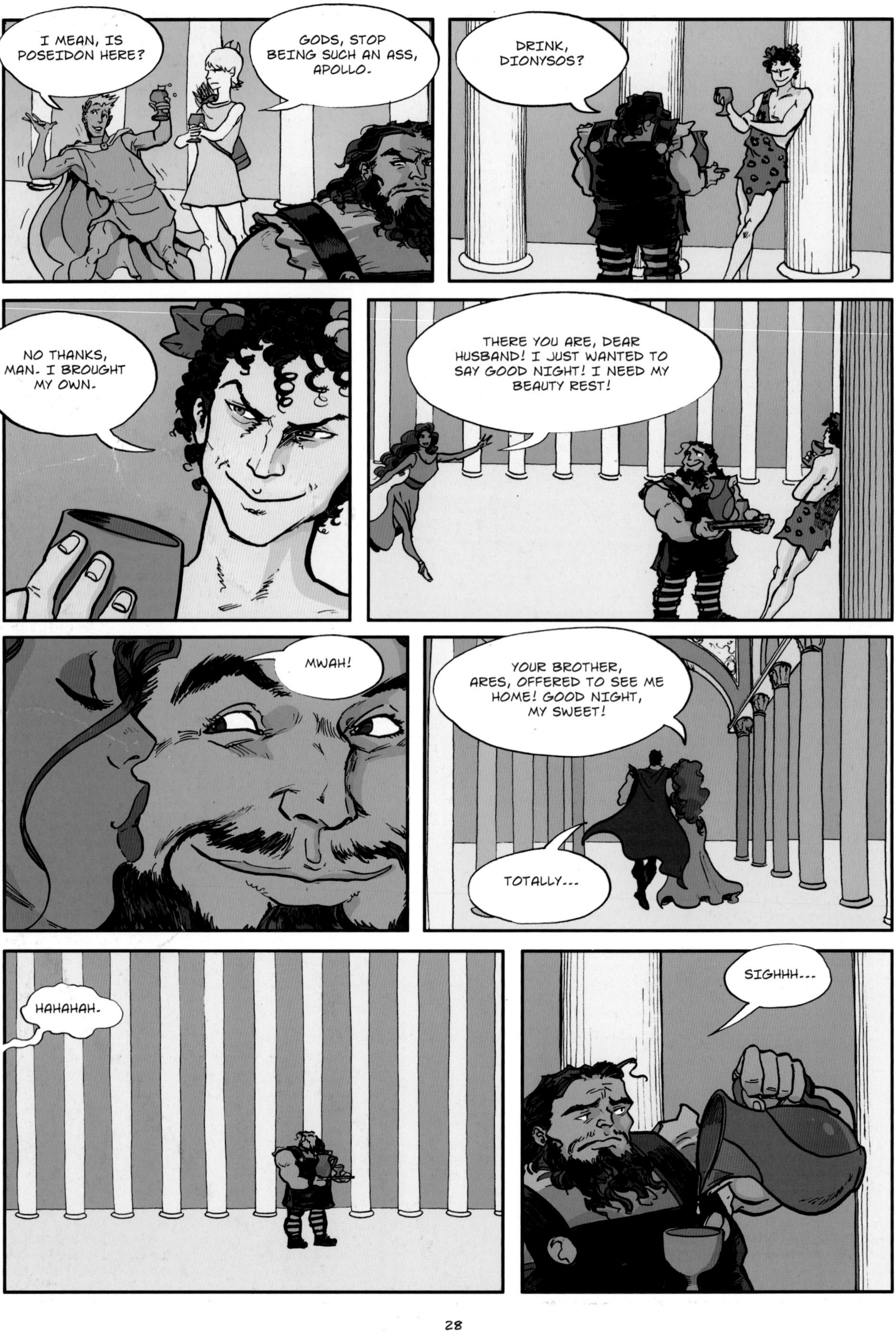
I MEAN, IS POSEIDON HERE?
GODS, STOP BEING SUCH AN ASS, APOLLO.
DRINK, DIONYSOS?
NO THANKS, MAN. I BROUGHT MY OWN.
THERE YOU ARE, DEAR HUSBAND! I JUST WANTED TO SAY GOOD NIGHT! I NEED MY BEAUTY REST!
MWAH!
YOUR BROTHER, ARES, OFFERED TO SEE ME HOME! GOOD NIGHT, MY SWEET!
TOTALLY...
HAHAHAH.
SIGHHH...

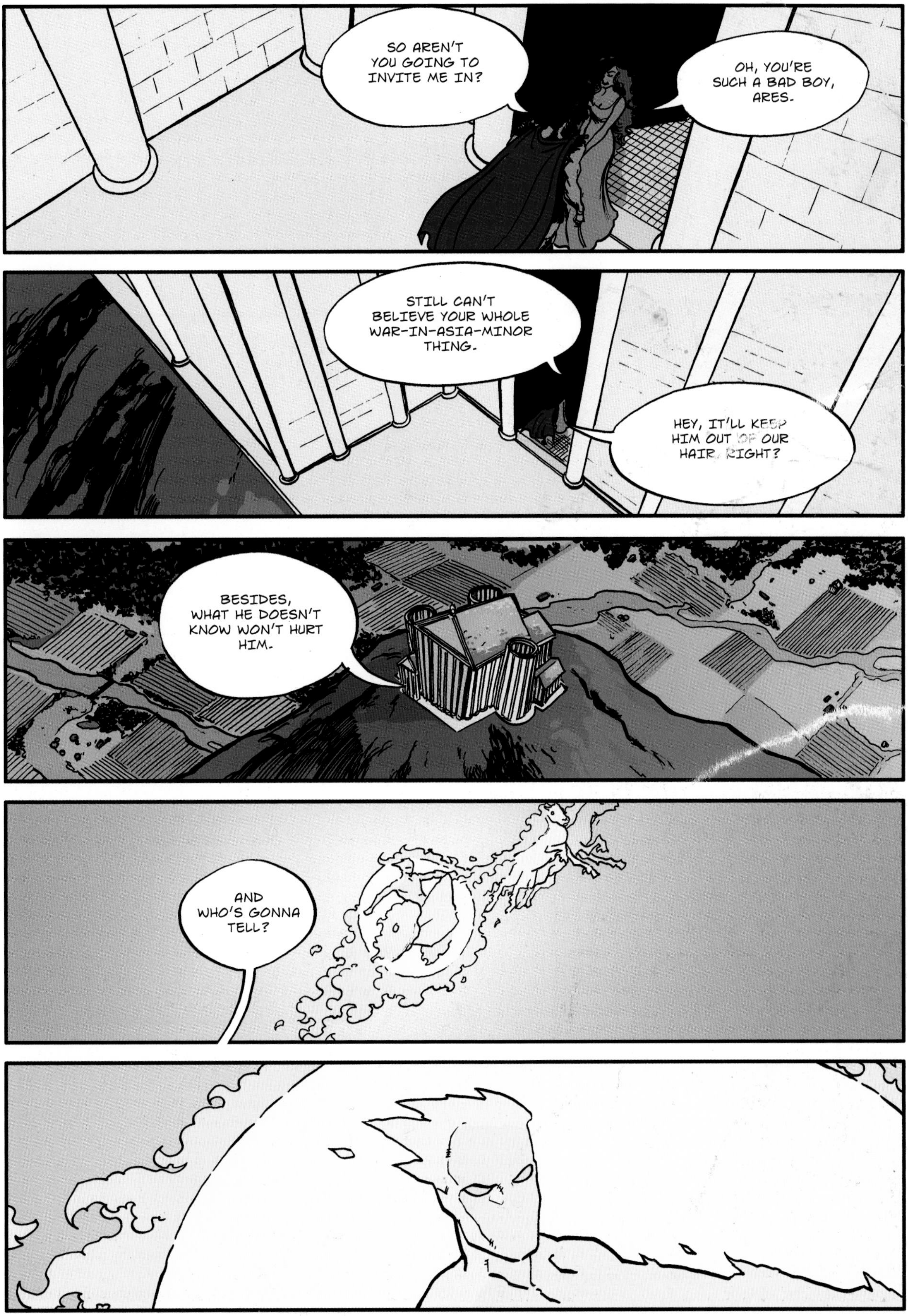
SO AREN'T YOU GOING TO INVITE ME IN?
OH, YOU'RE SUCH A BAD BOY, ARES.
STILL CAN'T BELIEVE YOUR WHOLE WAR-IN-ASIA-MINOR THING.
HEY, IT'LL KEEP HIM OUT OF OUR HAIR, RIGHT?
BESIDES, WHAT HE DOESN'T KNOW WON'T HURT HIM.
AND WHO'S GONNA TELL?

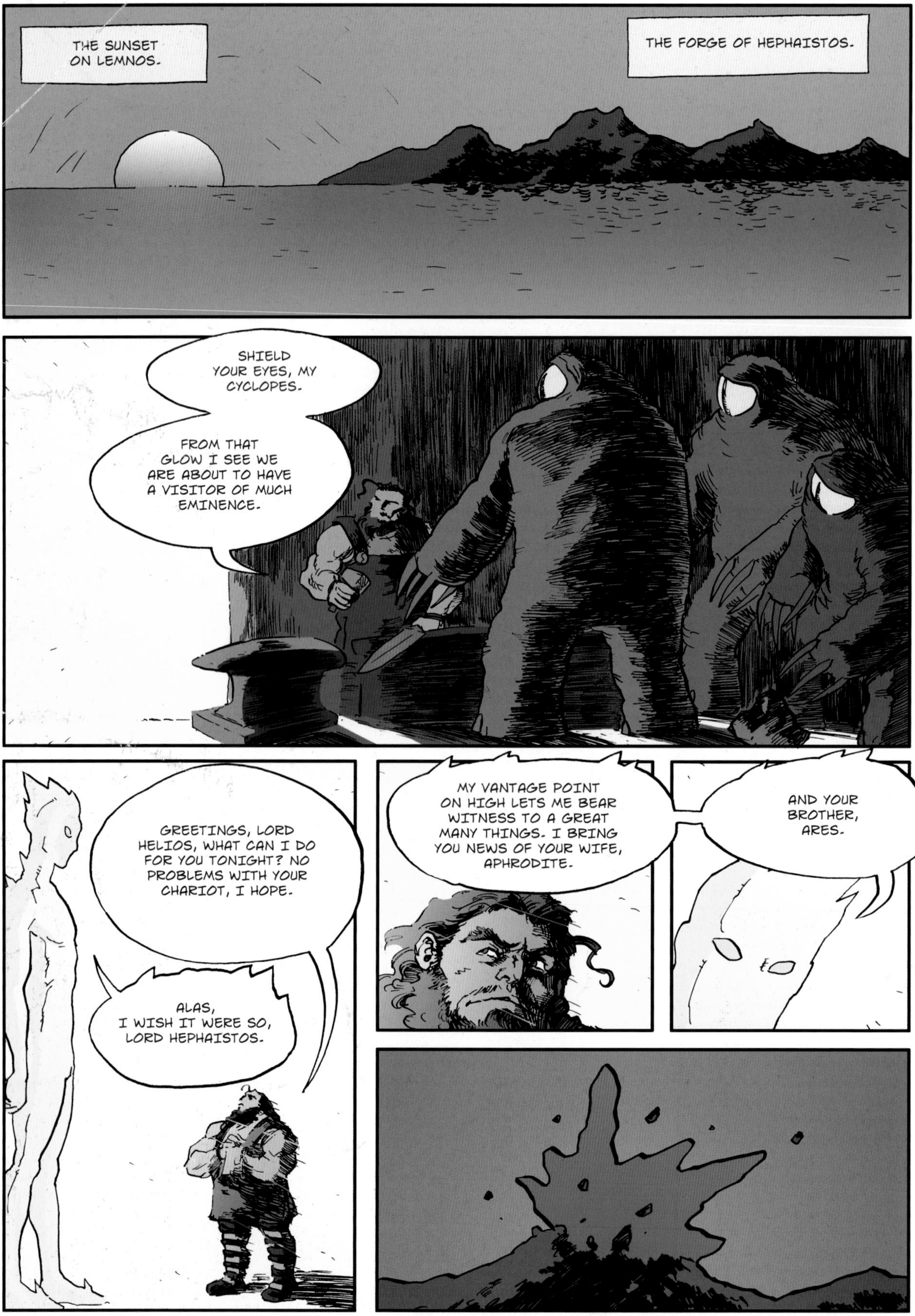
THE SUNSET ON LEMNOS.
THE FORGE OF HEPHAISTOS.
SHIELD YOUR EYES, MY CYCLOPES.
FROM THAT GLOW I SEE WE ARE ABOUT TO HAVE A VISITOR OF MUCH EMINENCE.
GREETINGS, LORD HELIOS, WHAT CAN I DO FOR YOU TONIGHT? NO PROBLEMS WITH YOUR CHARIOT, I HOPE.
ALAS, I WISH IT WERE SO, LORD HEPHAISTOS.
MY VANTAGE POINT ON HIGH LETS ME BEAR WITNESS TO A GREAT MANY THINGS. I BRING YOU NEWS OF YOUR WIFE, APHRODITE.
AND YOUR BROTHER, ARES.

THAT NIGHT.

ONCE THERE WAS A THIEF.

NOT A THIEF, A TITAN.

A TITAN WHO BRAVED THE COLD OF NIGHT.

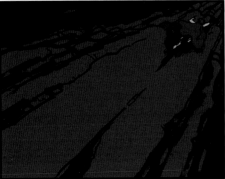

A TITAN WHO STORMED THE WALLS OF OLYMPUS.

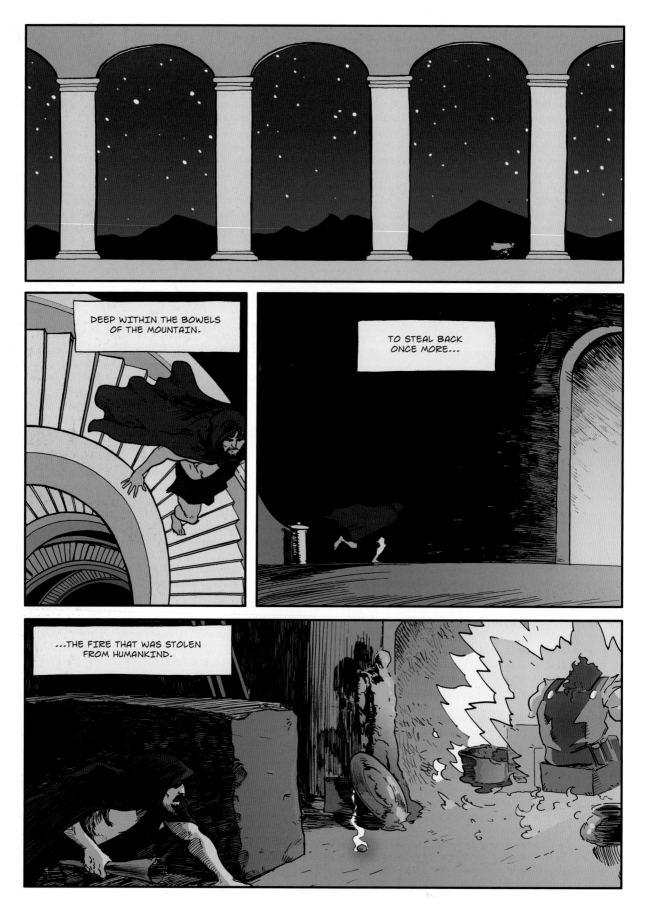

DEEP WITHIN THE BOWELS OF THE MOUNTAIN.

TO STEAL BACK ONCE MORE...

...THE FIRE THAT WAS STOLEN FROM HUMANKIND.

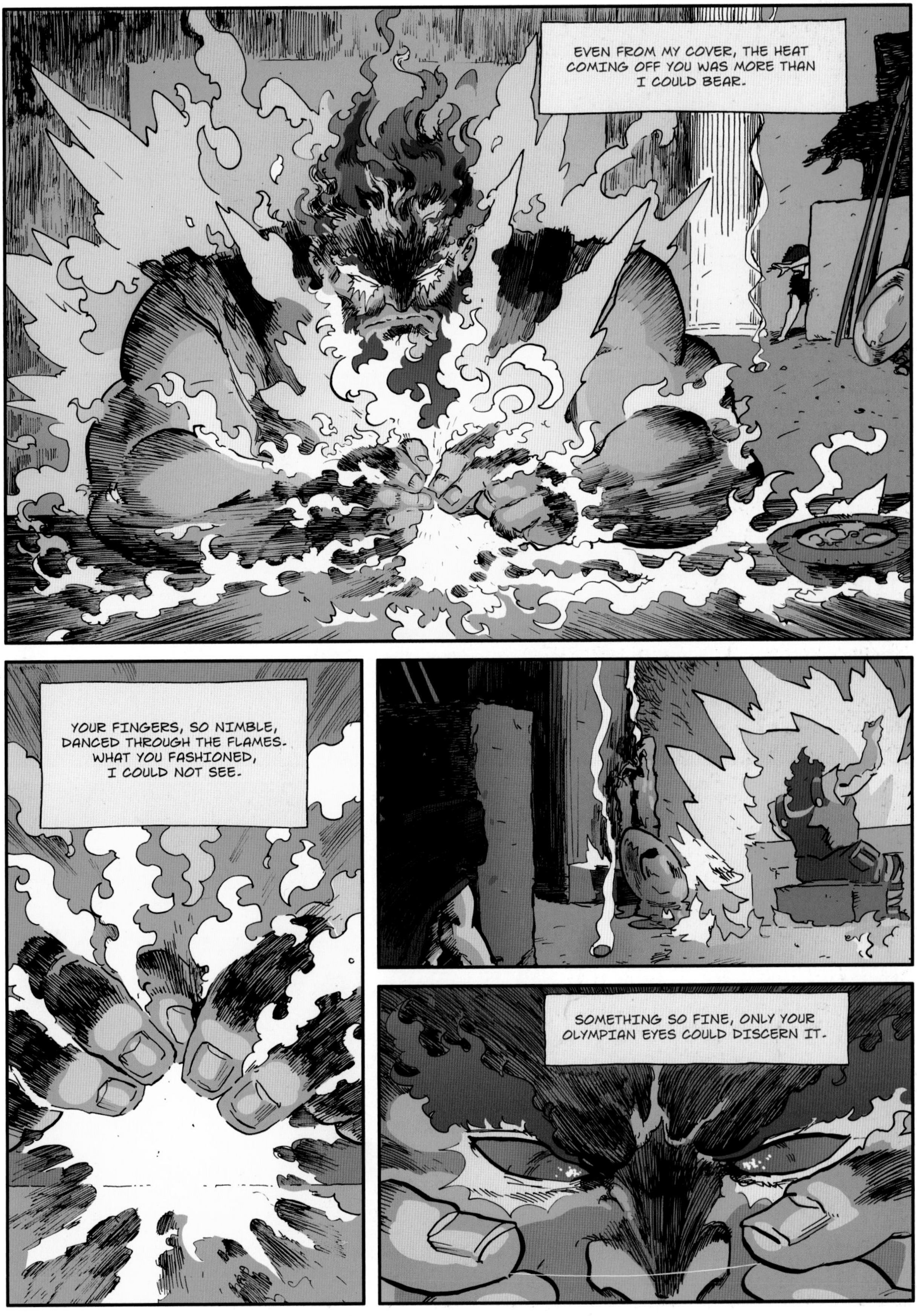
EVEN FROM MY COVER, THE HEAT COMING OFF YOU WAS MORE THAN I COULD BEAR.
YOUR FINGERS, SO NIMBLE, DANCED THROUGH THE FLAMES. WHAT YOU FASHIONED, I COULD NOT SEE.
SOMETHING SO FINE, ONLY YOUR OLYMPIAN EYES COULD DISCERN IT.

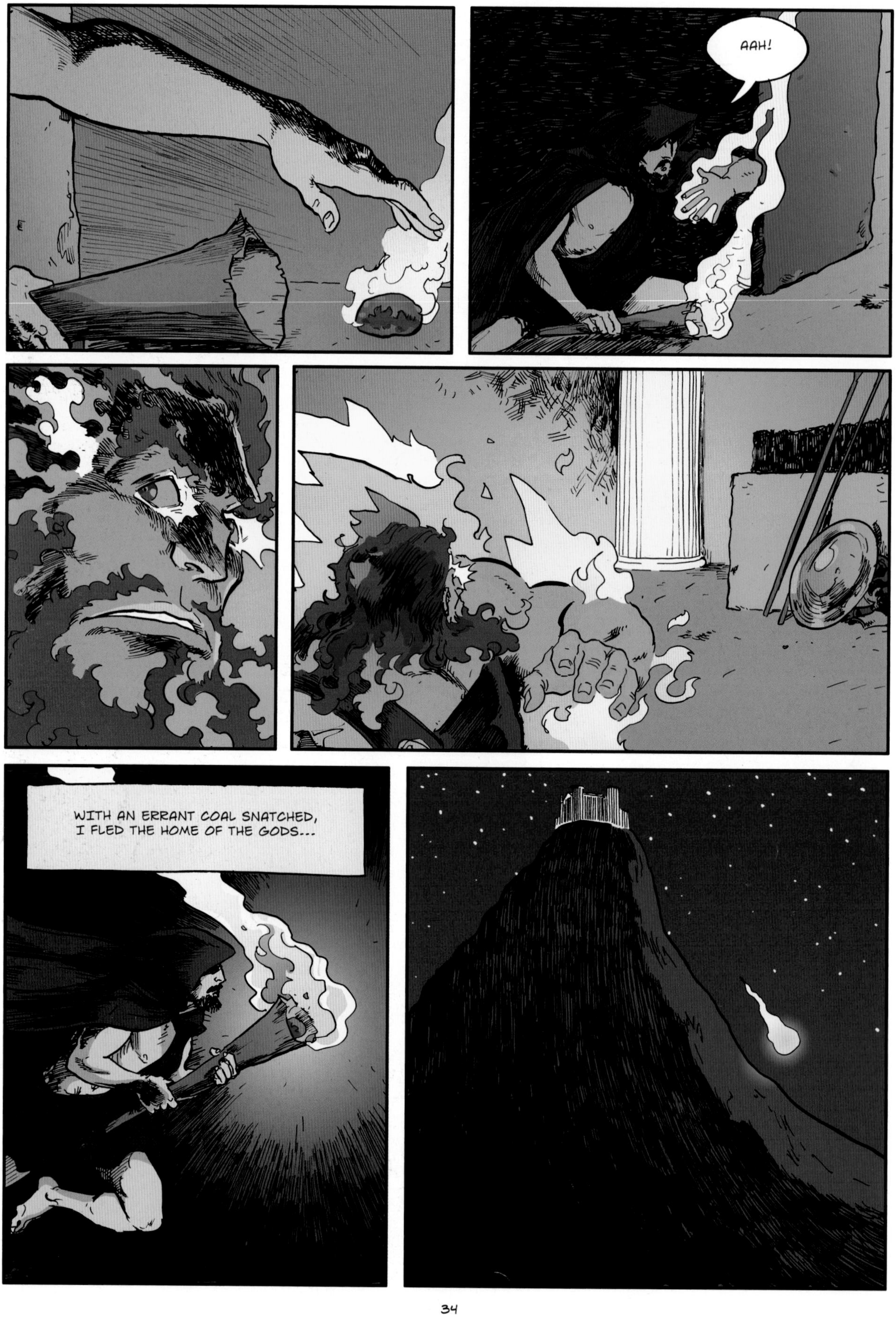
AAH!
WITH AN ERRANT COAL SNATCHED,
I FLED THE HOME OF THE GODS...

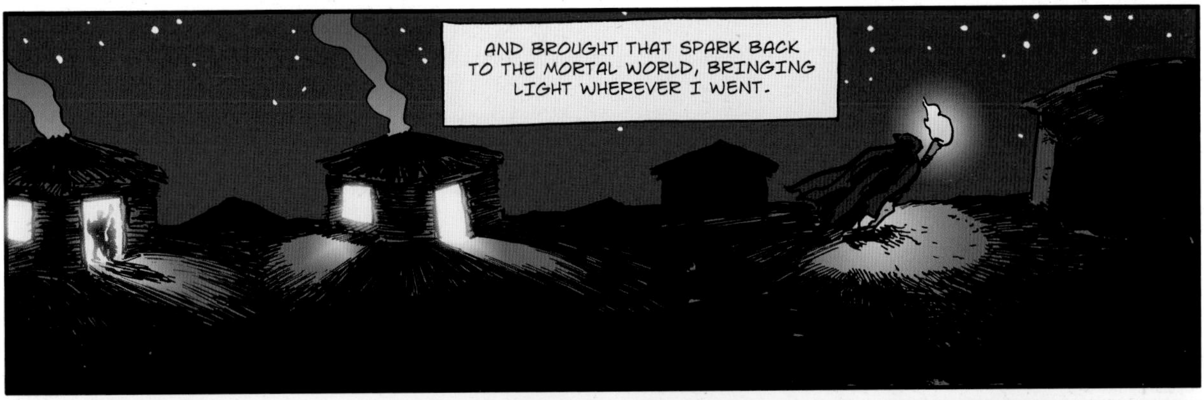
AND BROUGHT THAT SPARK BACK TO THE MORTAL WORLD, BRINGING LIGHT WHEREVER I WENT.

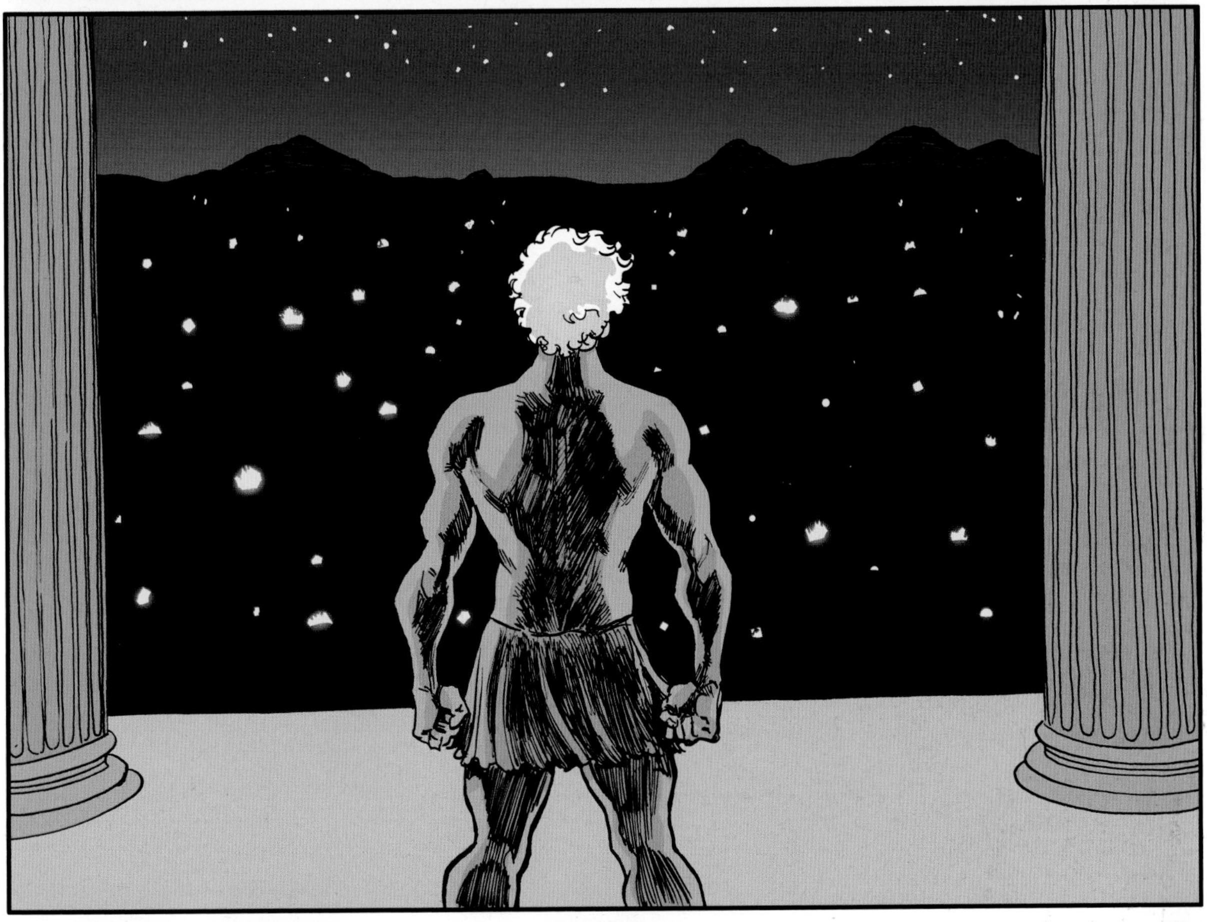

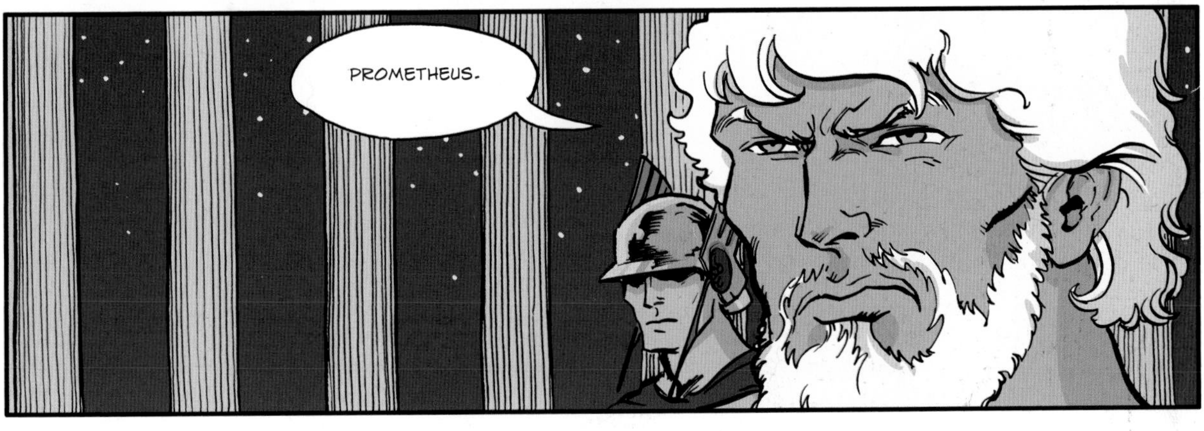
PROMETHEUS.

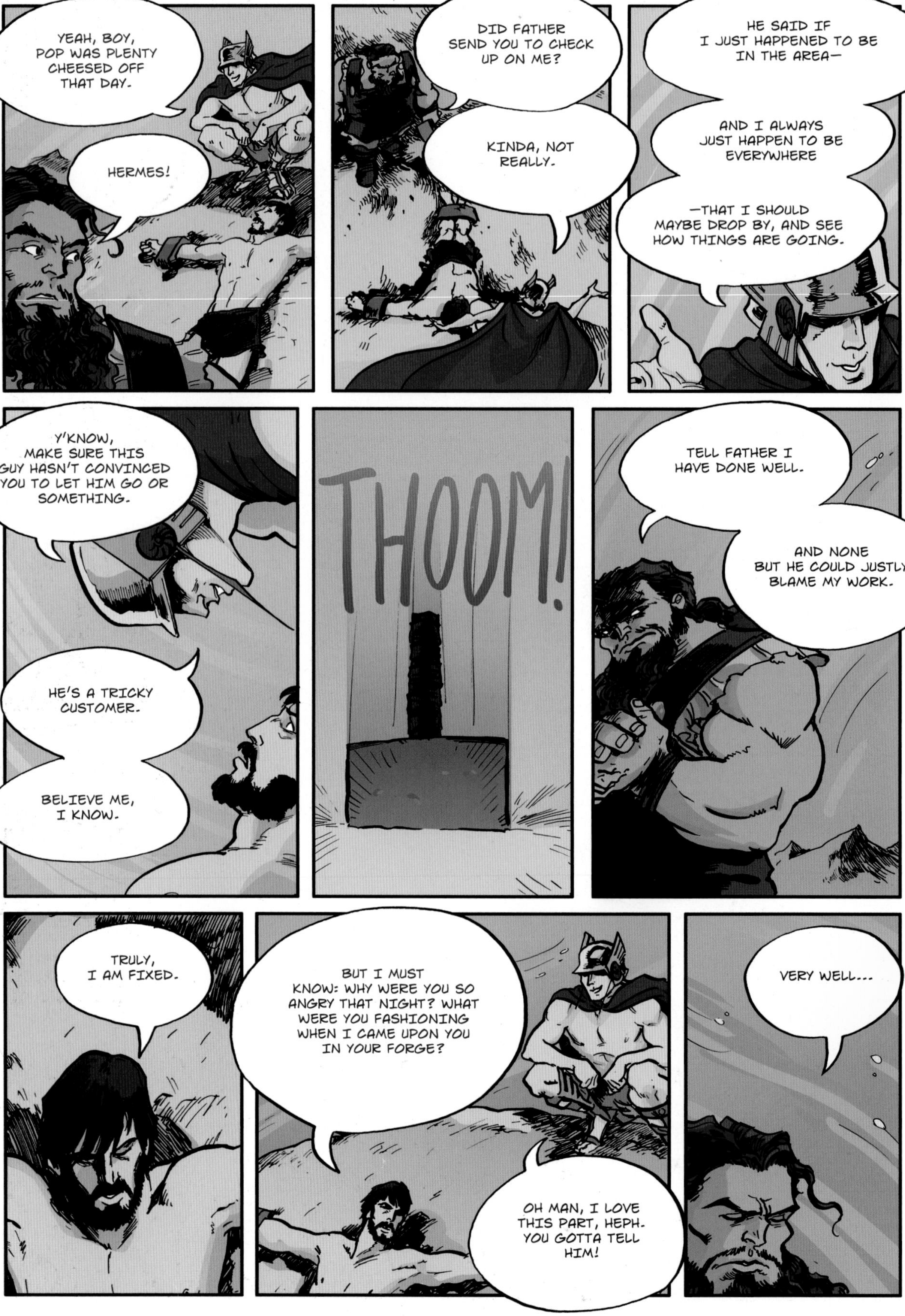
YEAH, BOY, POP WAS PLENTY CHEESED OFF THAT DAY.
HERMES!
DID FATHER SEND YOU TO CHECK UP ON ME?
KINDA, NOT REALLY.
HE SAID IF I JUST HAPPENED TO BE IN THE AREA—
AND I ALWAYS JUST HAPPEN TO BE EVERYWHERE
—THAT I SHOULD MAYBE DROP BY, AND SEE HOW THINGS ARE GOING.
Y'KNOW, MAKE SURE THIS GUY HASN'T CONVINCED YOU TO LET HIM GO OR SOMETHING.
HE'S A TRICKY CUSTOMER.
BELIEVE ME, I KNOW.
THOOM!
TELL FATHER I HAVE DONE WELL.
AND NONE BUT HE COULD JUSTLY BLAME MY WORK.
TRULY, I AM FIXED.
BUT I MUST KNOW: WHY WERE YOU SO ANGRY THAT NIGHT? WHAT WERE YOU FASHIONING WHEN I CAME UPON YOU IN YOUR FORGE?
OH MAN, I LOVE THIS PART, HEPH. YOU GOTTA TELL HIM!
VERY WELL...

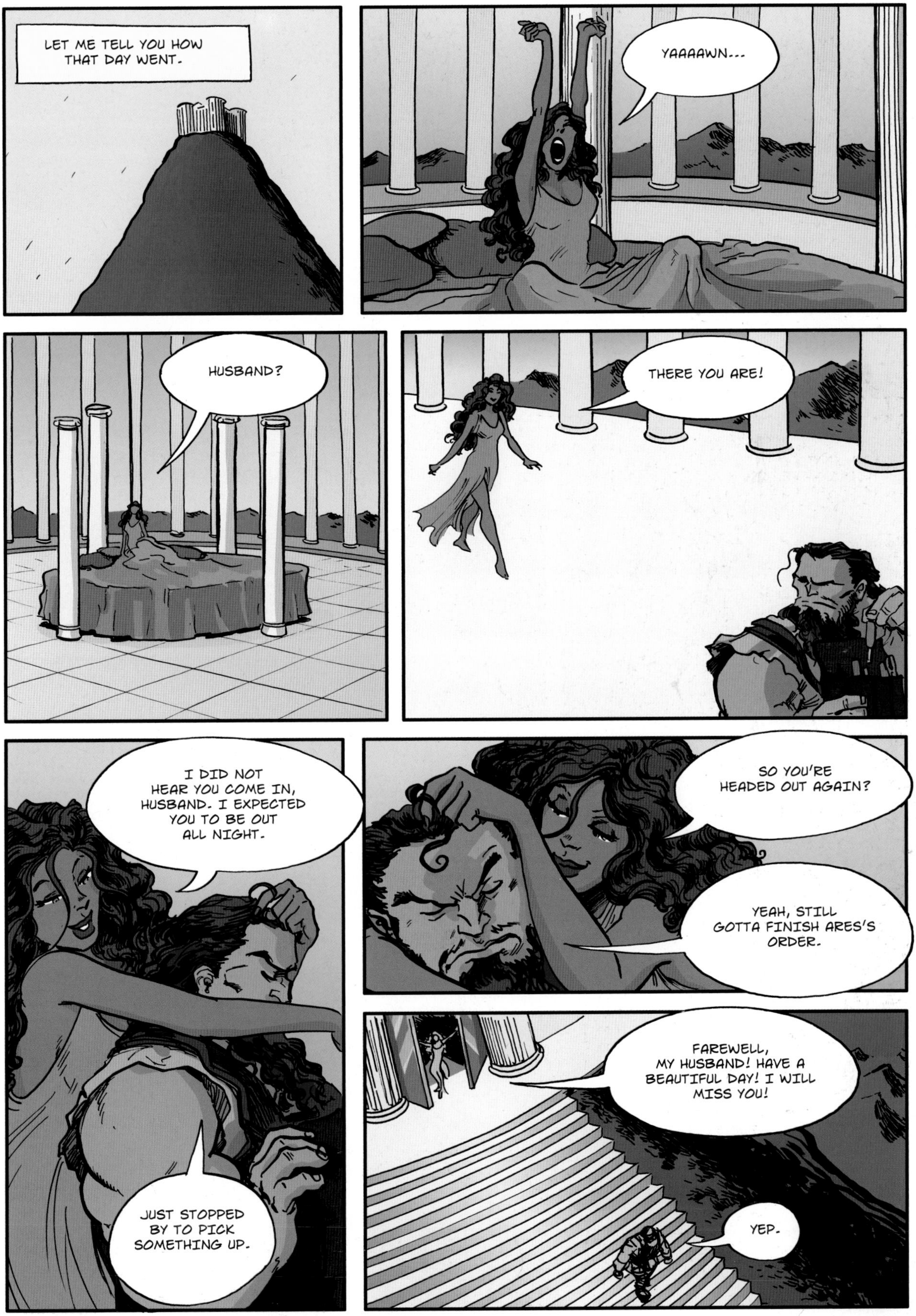
LET ME TELL YOU HOW THAT DAY WENT.
YAAAAWN...
HUSBAND?
THERE YOU ARE!
I DID NOT HEAR YOU COME IN, HUSBAND. I EXPECTED YOU TO BE OUT ALL NIGHT.
JUST STOPPED BY TO PICK SOMETHING UP.
SO YOU'RE HEADED OUT AGAIN?
YEAH, STILL GOTTA FINISH ARES'S ORDER.
FAREWELL, MY HUSBAND! HAVE A BEAUTIFUL DAY! I WILL MISS YOU!
YEP.

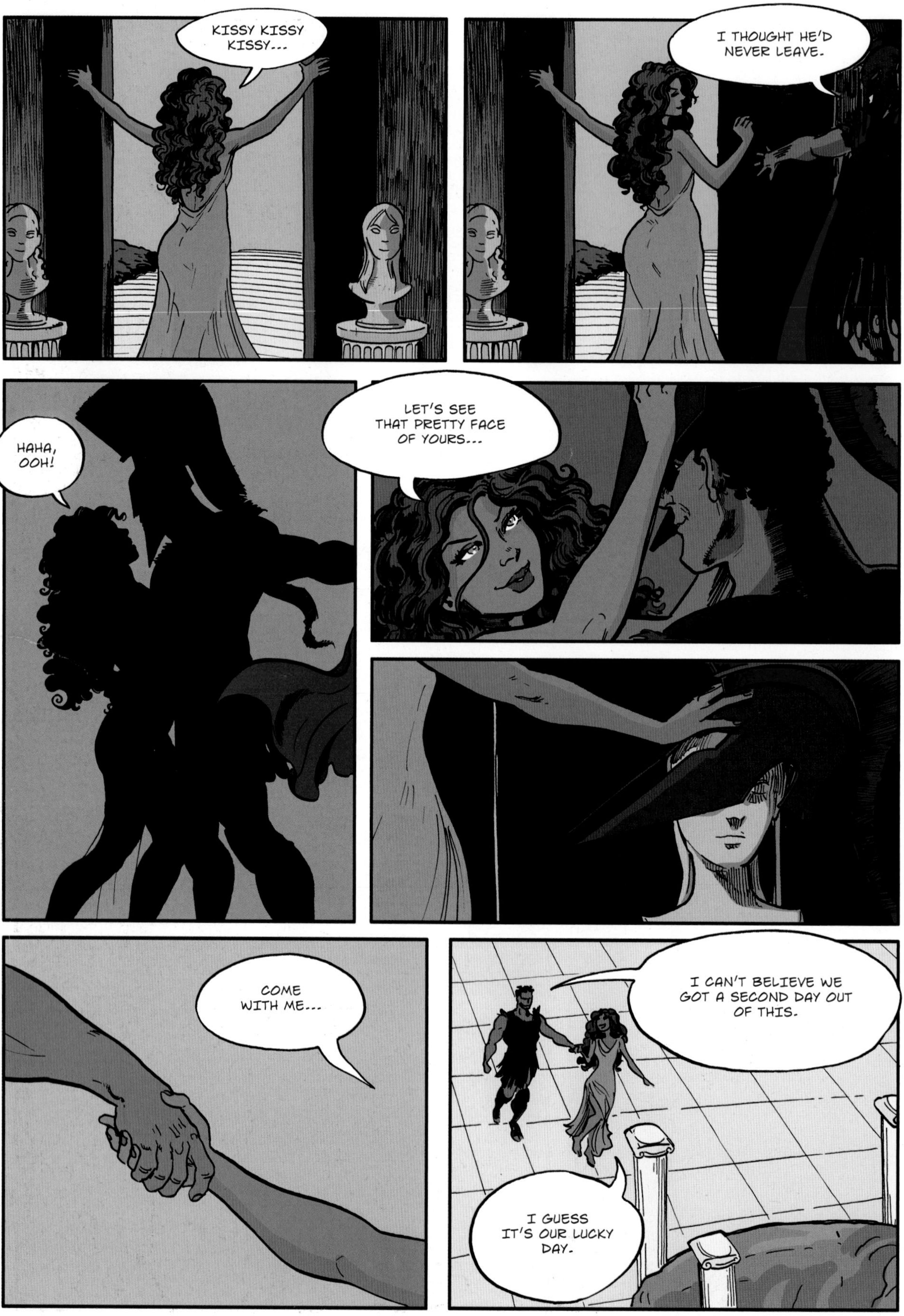
KISSY KISSY KISSY...
I THOUGHT HE'D NEVER LEAVE.
HAHA, OOH!
LET'S SEE THAT PRETTY FACE OF YOURS...
COME WITH ME...
I CAN'T BELIEVE WE GOT A SECOND DAY OUT OF THIS.
I GUESS IT'S OUR LUCKY DAY.

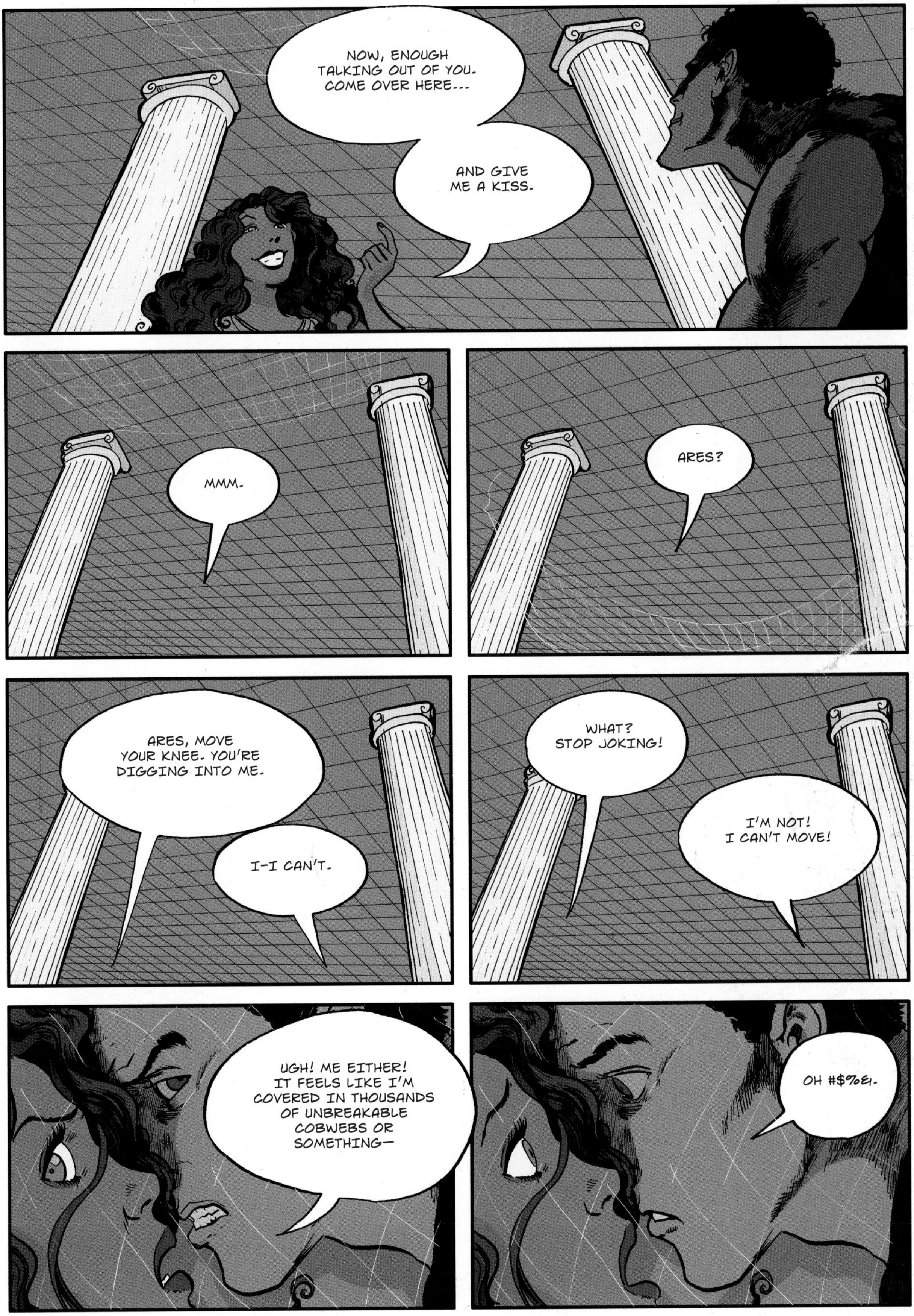
NOW, ENOUGH TALKING OUT OF YOU. COME OVER HERE...
AND GIVE ME A KISS.
MMM.
ARES?
ARES, MOVE YOUR KNEE. YOU'RE DIGGING INTO ME.
I-I CAN'T.
WHAT? STOP JOKING!
I'M NOT! I CAN'T MOVE!
UGH! ME EITHER! IT FEELS LIKE I'M COVERED IN THOUSANDS OF UNBREAKABLE COBWEBS OR SOMETHING—
OH #$%&!.

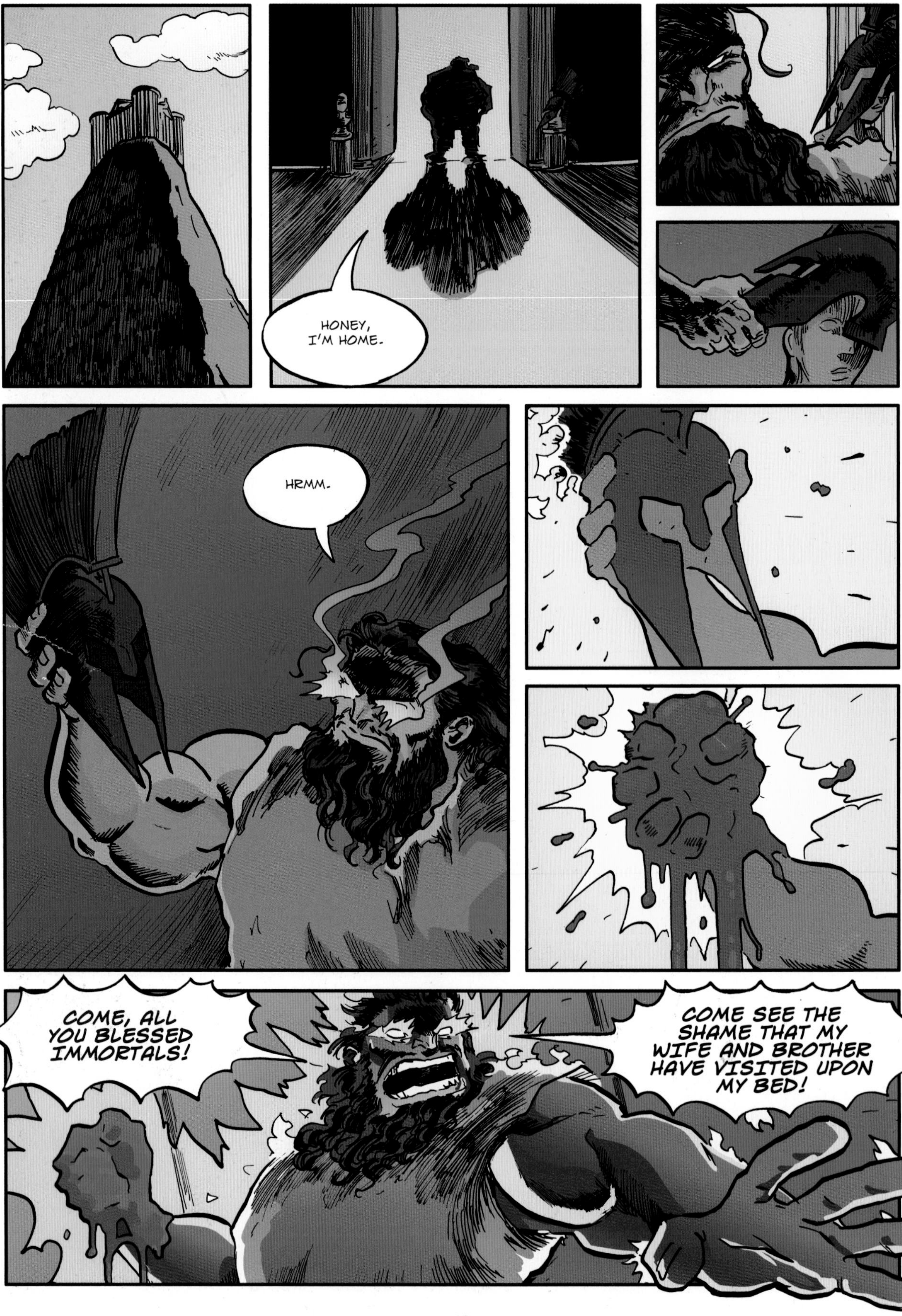
HONEY, I'M HOME.
HRMM.
COME, ALL YOU BLESSED IMMORTALS!
COME SEE THE SHAME THAT MY WIFE AND BROTHER HAVE VISITED UPON MY BED!

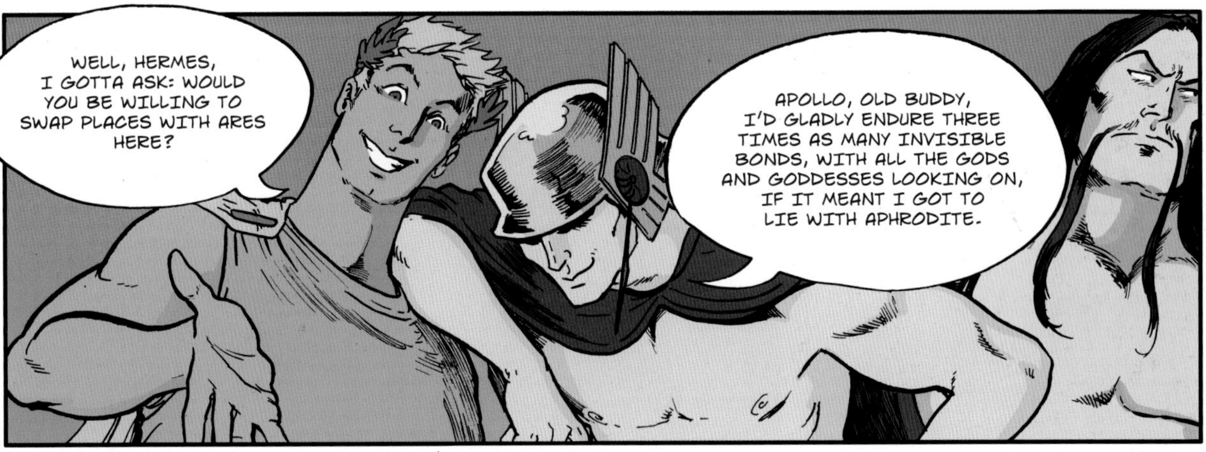
WELL, HERMES, I GOTTA ASK: WOULD YOU BE WILLING TO SWAP PLACES WITH ARES HERE?
APOLLO, OLD BUDDY, I'D GLADLY ENDURE THREE TIMES AS MANY INVISIBLE BONDS, WITH ALL THE GODS AND GODDESSES LOOKING ON, IF IT MEANT I GOT TO LIE WITH APHRODITE.

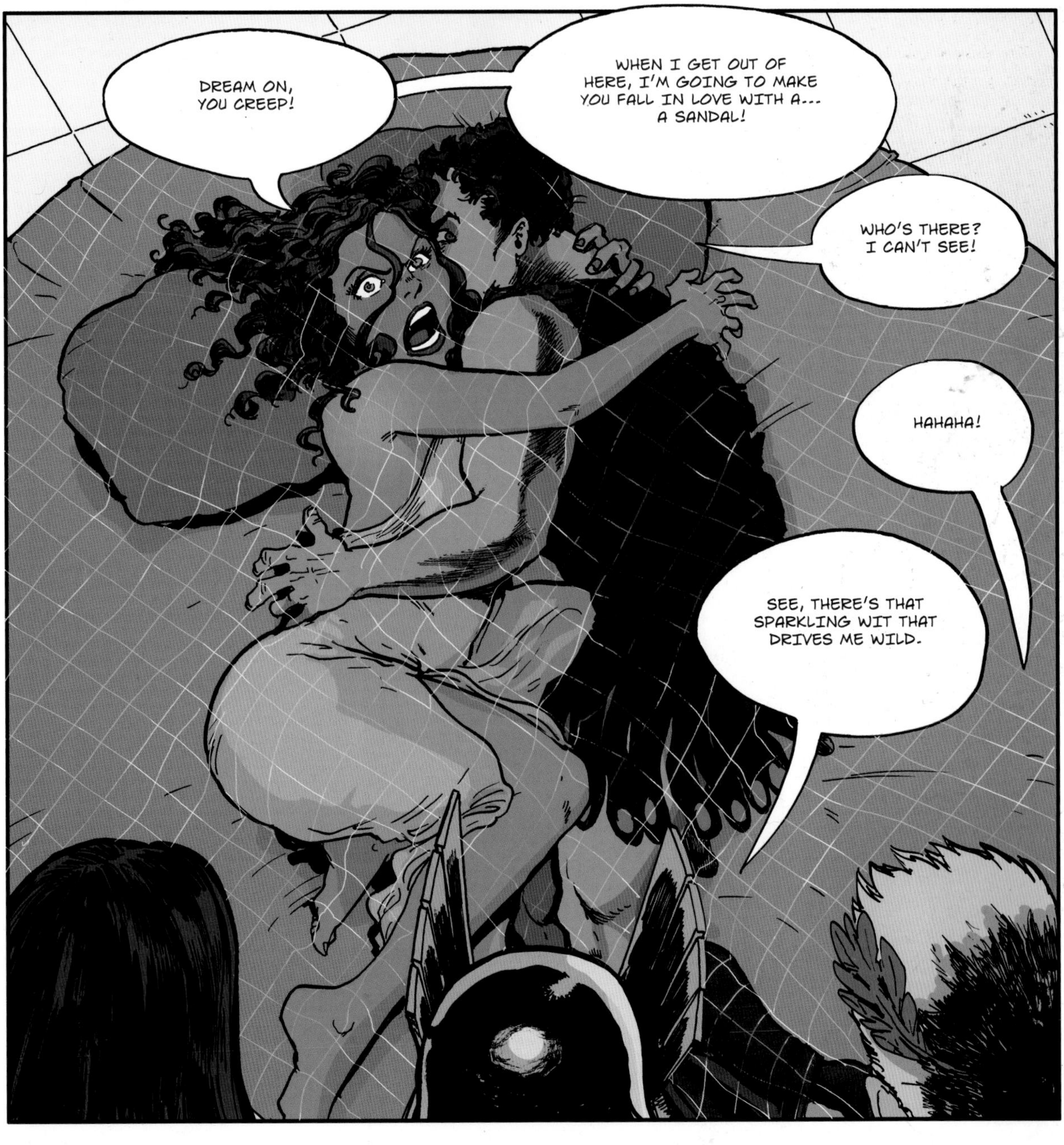
DREAM ON, YOU CREEP!
WHEN I GET OUT OF HERE, I'M GOING TO MAKE YOU FALL IN LOVE WITH A... A SANDAL!
WHO'S THERE? I CAN'T SEE!
HAHAHA!
SEE, THERE'S THAT SPARKLING WIT THAT DRIVES ME WILD.

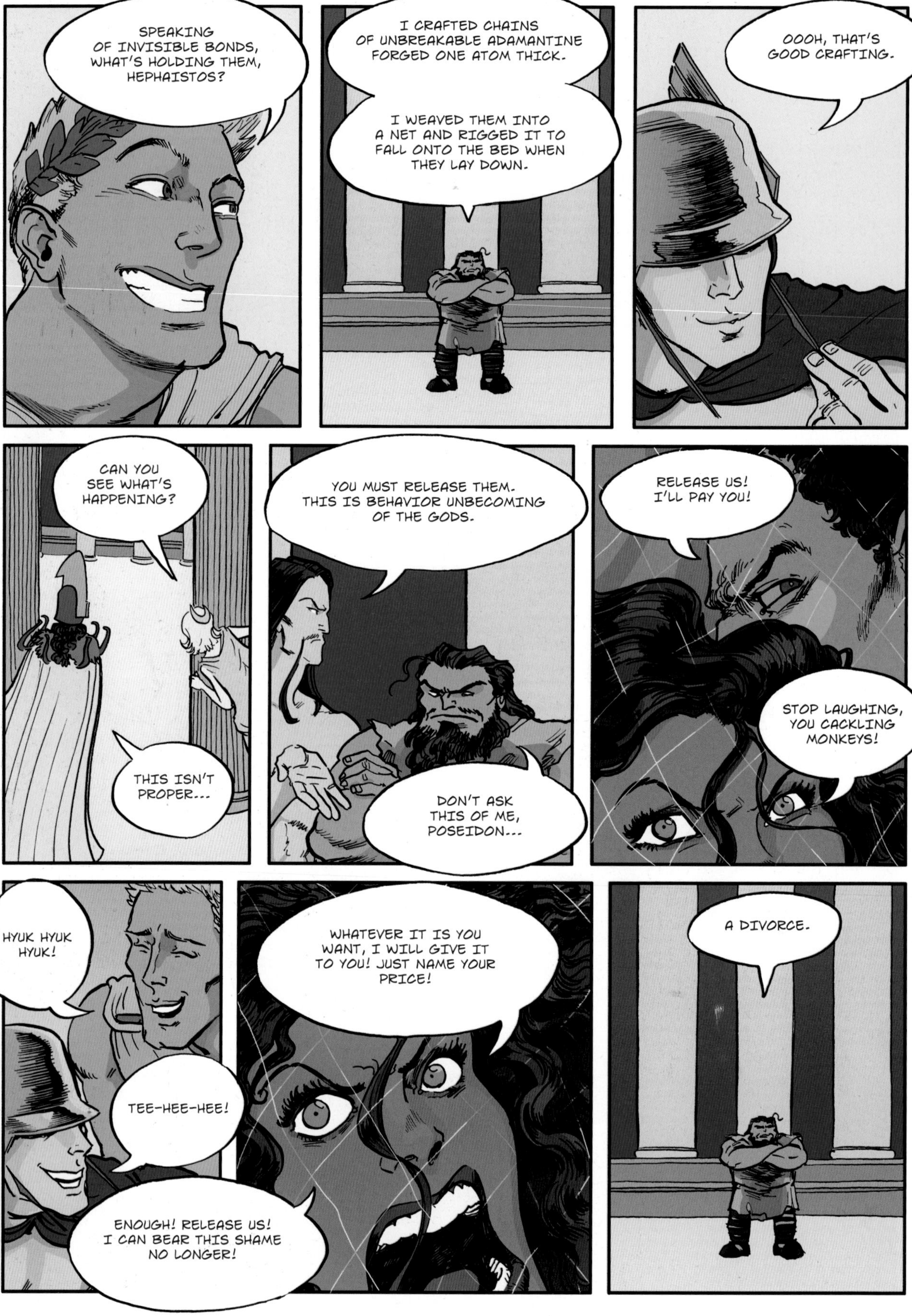

SPEAKING OF INVISIBLE BONDS, WHAT'S HOLDING THEM, HEPHAISTOS?
I CRAFTED CHAINS OF UNBREAKABLE ADAMANTINE FORGED ONE ATOM THICK.
I WEAVED THEM INTO A NET AND RIGGED IT TO FALL ONTO THE BED WHEN THEY LAY DOWN.
OOOH, THAT'S GOOD CRAFTING.
CAN YOU SEE WHAT'S HAPPENING?
THIS ISN'T PROPER...
YOU MUST RELEASE THEM. THIS IS BEHAVIOR UNBECOMING OF THE GODS.
DON'T ASK THIS OF ME, POSEIDON...
RELEASE US! I'LL PAY YOU!
STOP LAUGHING, YOU CACKLING MONKEYS!
HYUK HYUK HYUK!
TEE-HEE-HEE!
ENOUGH! RELEASE US! I CAN BEAR THIS SHAME NO LONGER!
WHATEVER IT IS YOU WANT, I WILL GIVE IT TO YOU! JUST NAME YOUR PRICE!
A DIVORCE.

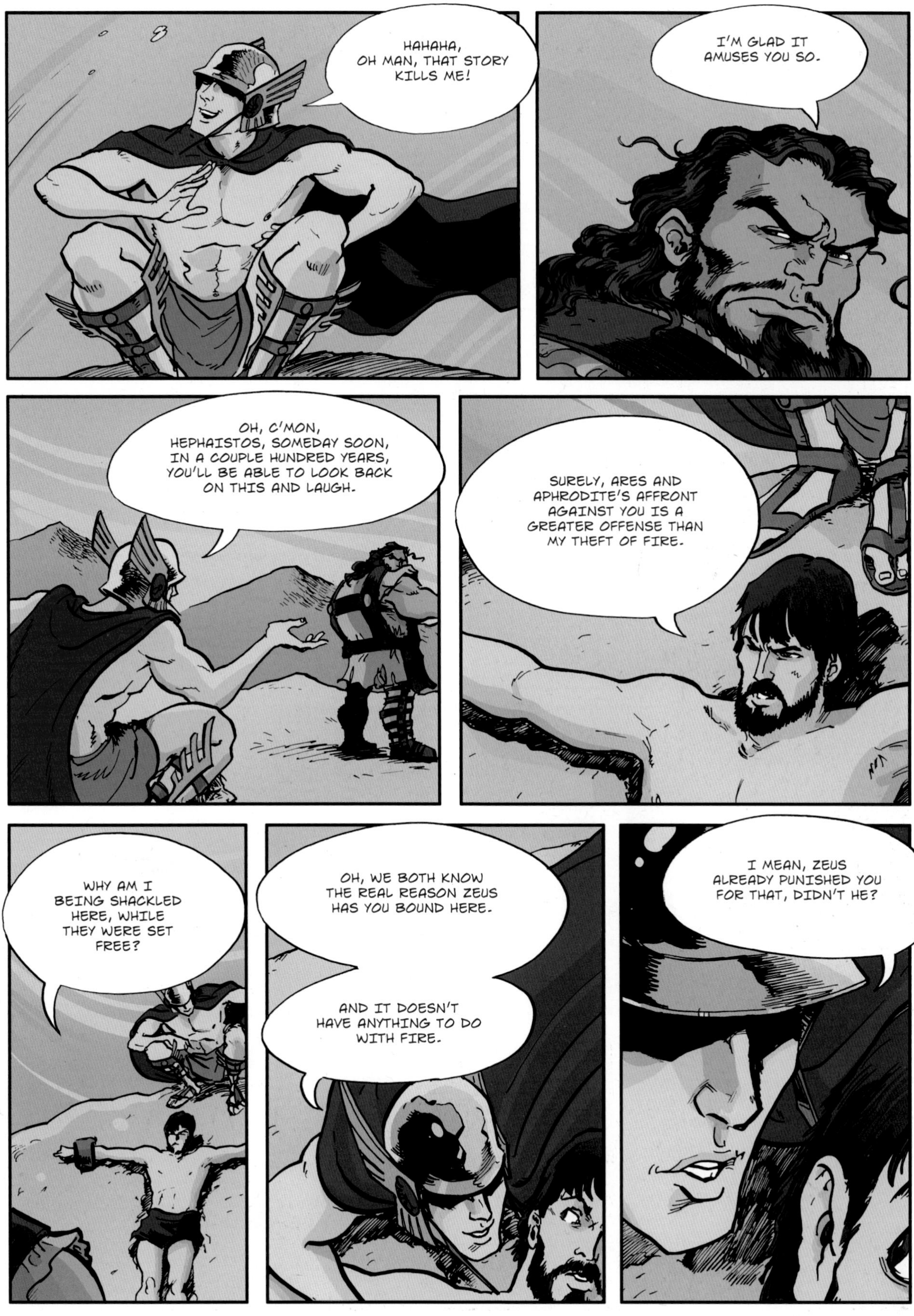
HAHAHA, OH MAN, THAT STORY KILLS ME!
I'M GLAD IT AMUSES YOU SO.
OH, C'MON, HEPHAISTOS, SOMEDAY SOON, IN A COUPLE HUNDRED YEARS, YOU'LL BE ABLE TO LOOK BACK ON THIS AND LAUGH.
SURELY, ARES AND APHRODITE'S AFFRONT AGAINST YOU IS A GREATER OFFENSE THAN MY THEFT OF FIRE.
WHY AM I BEING SHACKLED HERE, WHILE THEY WERE SET FREE?
OH, WE BOTH KNOW THE REAL REASON ZEUS HAS YOU BOUND HERE.
AND IT DOESN'T HAVE ANYTHING TO DO WITH FIRE.
I MEAN, ZEUS ALREADY PUNISHED YOU FOR THAT, DIDN'T HE?

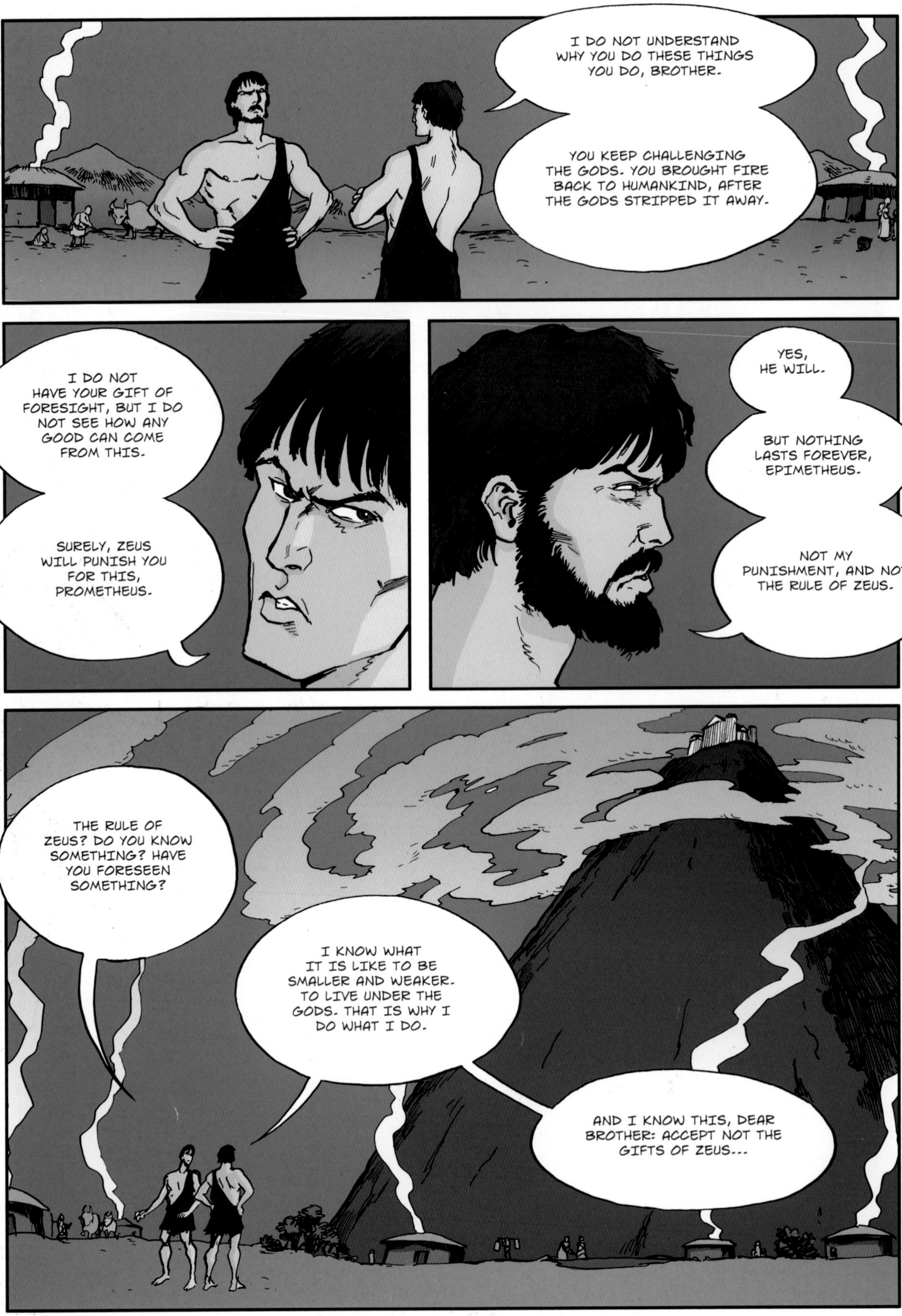
I DO NOT UNDERSTAND WHY YOU DO THESE THINGS YOU DO, BROTHER.
YOU KEEP CHALLENGING THE GODS. YOU BROUGHT FIRE BACK TO HUMANKIND, AFTER THE GODS STRIPPED IT AWAY.
I DO NOT HAVE YOUR GIFT OF FORESIGHT, BUT I DO NOT SEE HOW ANY GOOD CAN COME FROM THIS.
SURELY, ZEUS WILL PUNISH YOU FOR THIS, PROMETHEUS.
YES, HE WILL.
BUT NOTHING LASTS FOREVER, EPIMETHEUS.
NOT MY PUNISHMENT, AND NOT THE RULE OF ZEUS.
THE RULE OF ZEUS? DO YOU KNOW SOMETHING? HAVE YOU FORESEEN SOMETHING?
I KNOW WHAT IT IS LIKE TO BE SMALLER AND WEAKER. TO LIVE UNDER THE GODS. THAT IS WHY I DO WHAT I DO.
AND I KNOW THIS, DEAR BROTHER: ACCEPT NOT THE GIFTS OF ZEUS...

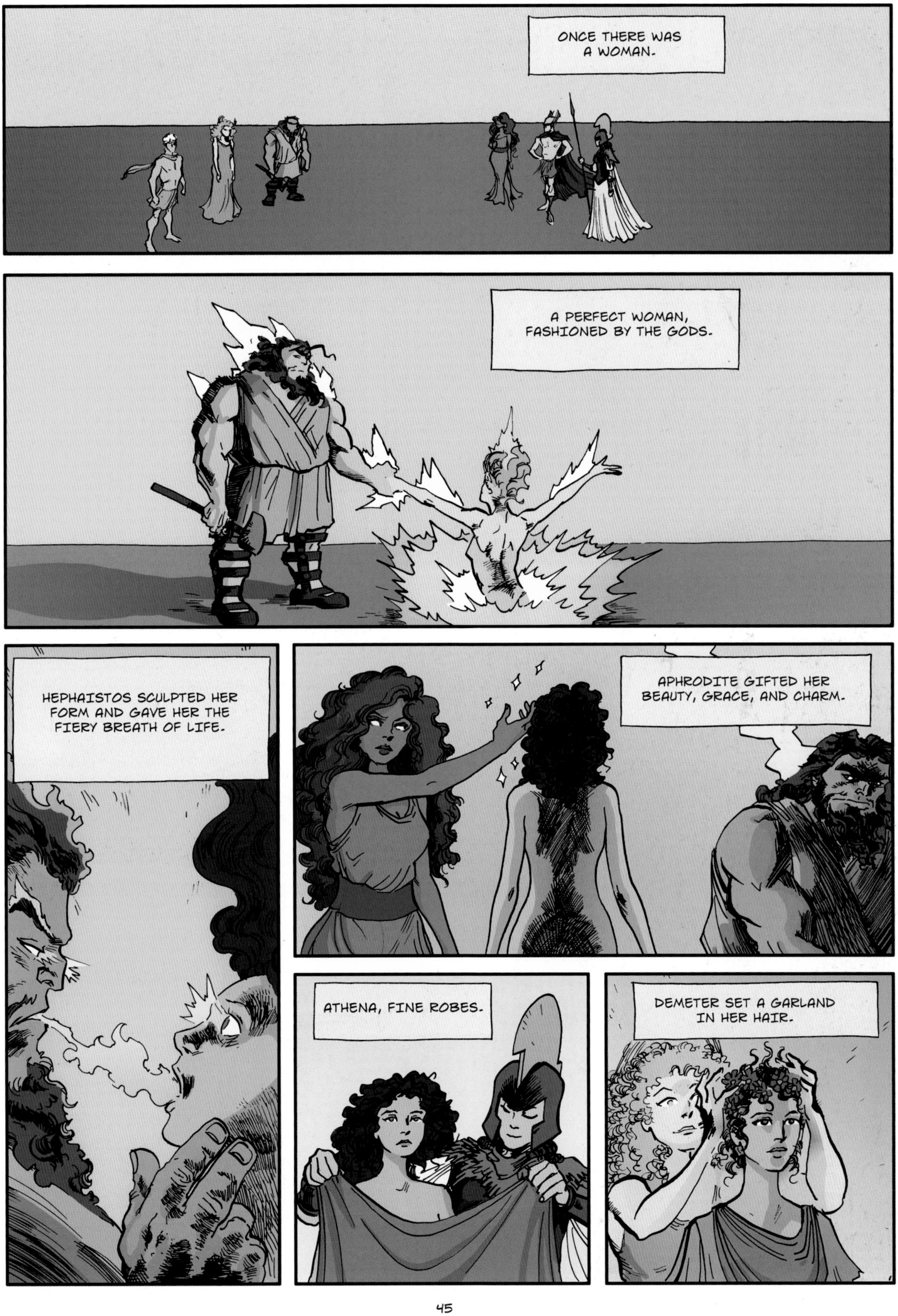

ONCE THERE WAS A WOMAN.
A PERFECT WOMAN, FASHIONED BY THE GODS.
HEPHAISTOS SCULPTED HER FORM AND GAVE HER THE FIERY BREATH OF LIFE.
APHRODITE GIFTED HER BEAUTY, GRACE, AND CHARM.
ATHENA, FINE ROBES.
DEMETER SET A GARLAND IN HER HAIR.

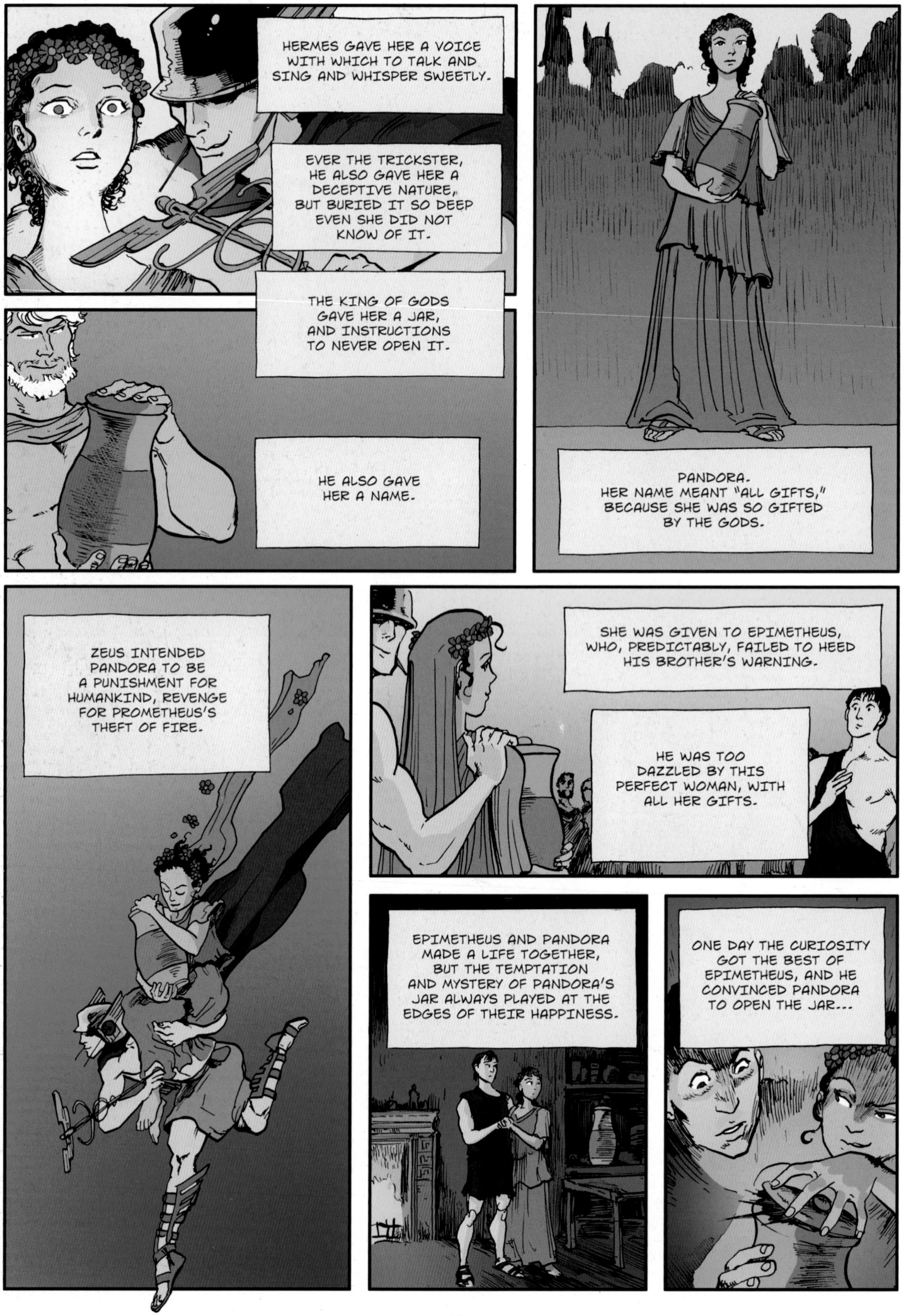
HERMES GAVE HER A VOICE WITH WHICH TO TALK AND SING AND WHISPER SWEETLY.
EVER THE TRICKSTER, HE ALSO GAVE HER A DECEPTIVE NATURE, BUT BURIED IT SO DEEP EVEN SHE DID NOT KNOW OF IT.
THE KING OF GODS GAVE HER A JAR, AND INSTRUCTIONS TO NEVER OPEN IT.
HE ALSO GAVE HER A NAME.
PANDORA. HER NAME MEANT "ALL GIFTS," BECAUSE SHE WAS SO GIFTED BY THE GODS.
ZEUS INTENDED PANDORA TO BE A PUNISHMENT FOR HUMANKIND, REVENGE FOR PROMETHEUS'S THEFT OF FIRE.
SHE WAS GIVEN TO EPIMETHEUS, WHO, PREDICTABLY, FAILED TO HEED HIS BROTHER'S WARNING.
HE WAS TOO DAZZLED BY THIS PERFECT WOMAN, WITH ALL HER GIFTS.
EPIMETHEUS AND PANDORA MADE A LIFE TOGETHER, BUT THE TEMPTATION AND MYSTERY OF PANDORA'S JAR ALWAYS PLAYED AT THE EDGES OF THEIR HAPPINESS.
ONE DAY THE CURIOSITY GOT THE BEST OF EPIMETHEUS, AND HE CONVINCED PANDORA TO OPEN THE JAR...

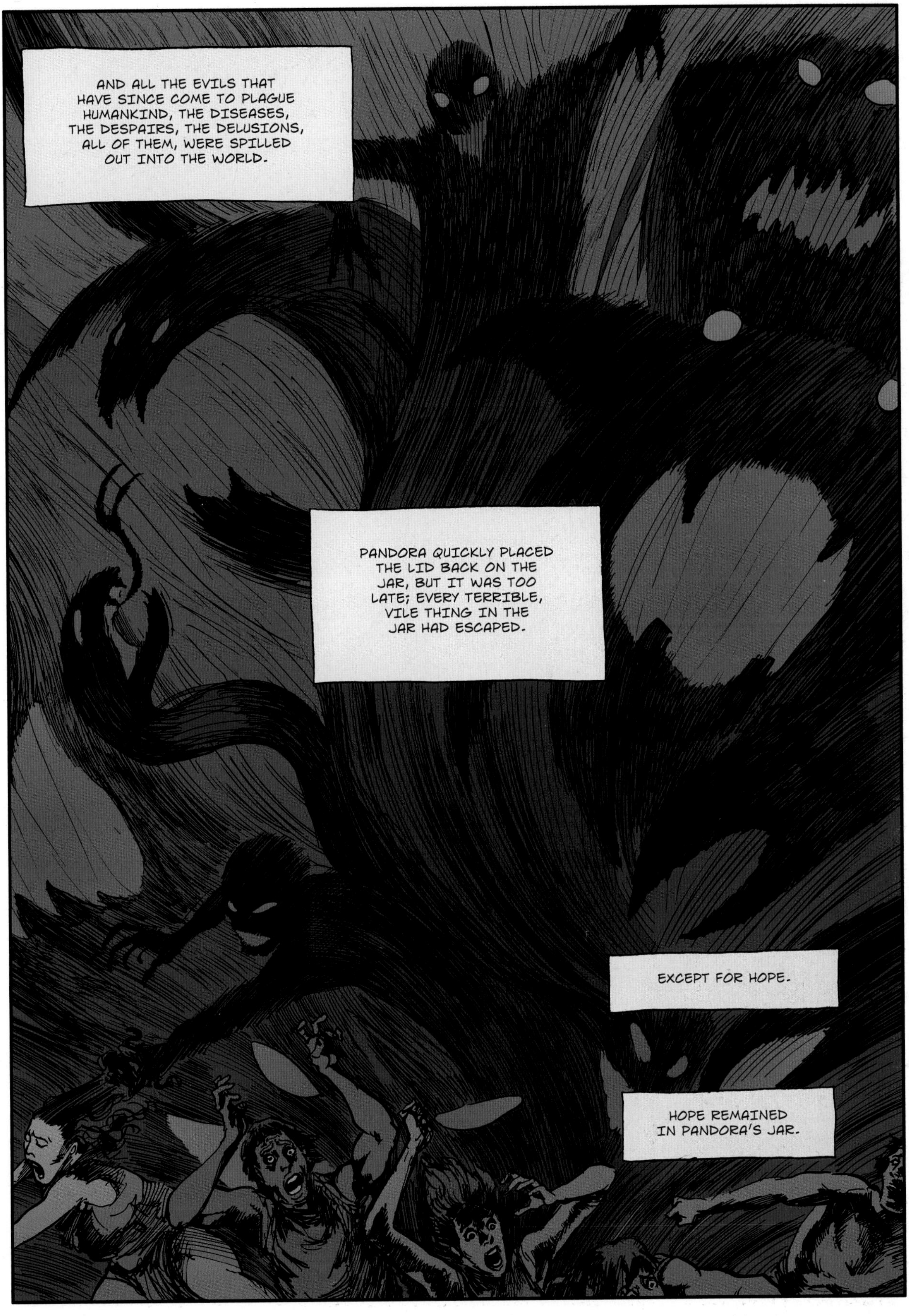
AND ALL THE EVILS THAT HAVE SINCE COME TO PLAGUE HUMANKIND, THE DISEASES, THE DESPAIRS, THE DELUSIONS, ALL OF THEM, WERE SPILLED OUT INTO THE WORLD.
PANDORA QUICKLY PLACED THE LID BACK ON THE JAR, BUT IT WAS TOO LATE; EVERY TERRIBLE, VILE THING IN THE JAR HAD ESCAPED.
EXCEPT FOR HOPE.
HOPE REMAINED IN PANDORA'S JAR.

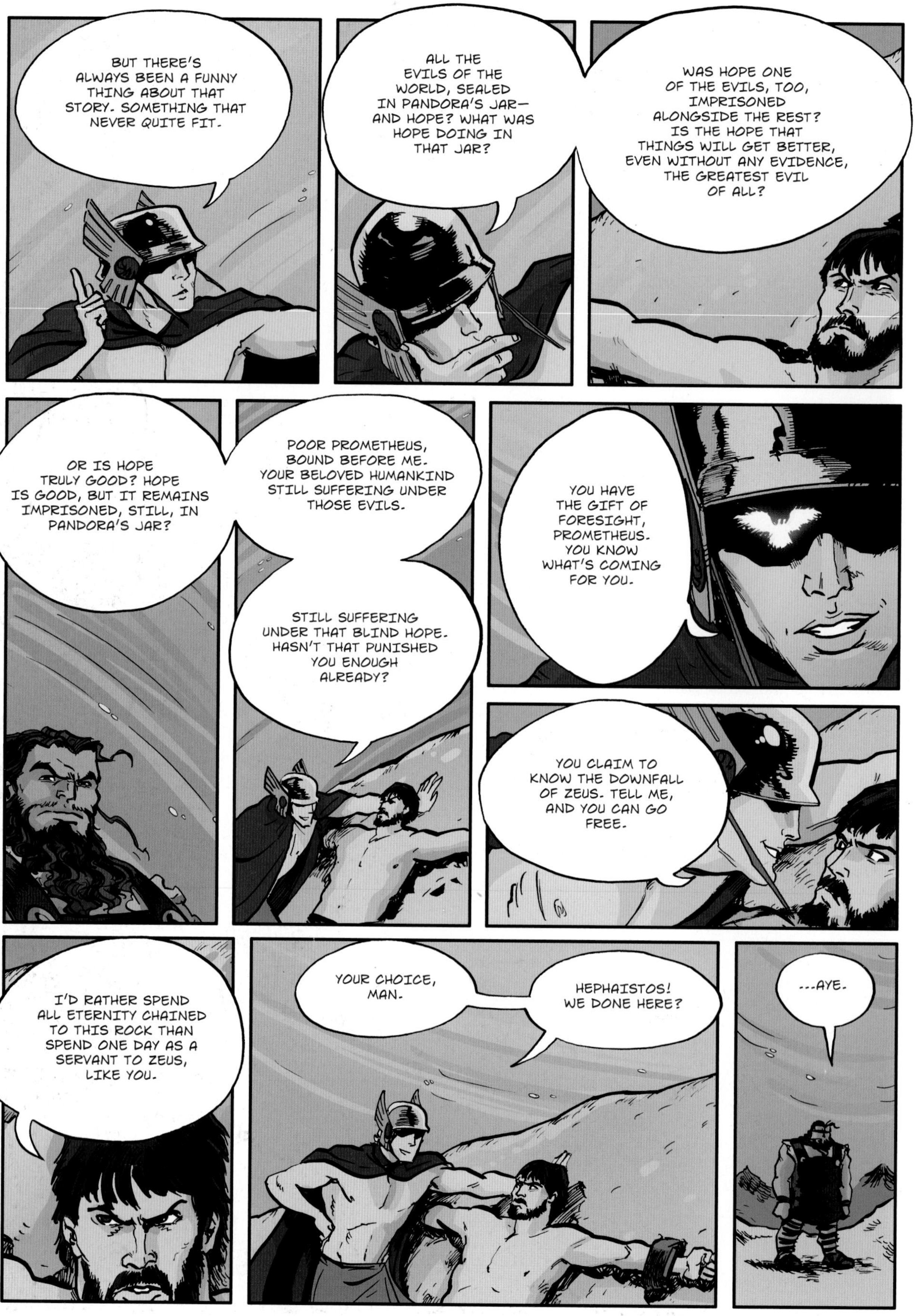
BUT THERE'S ALWAYS BEEN A FUNNY THING ABOUT THAT STORY. SOMETHING THAT NEVER QUITE FIT.
ALL THE EVILS OF THE WORLD, SEALED IN PANDORA'S JAR—AND HOPE? WHAT WAS HOPE DOING IN THAT JAR?
WAS HOPE ONE OF THE EVILS, TOO, IMPRISONED ALONGSIDE THE REST? IS THE HOPE THAT THINGS WILL GET BETTER, EVEN WITHOUT ANY EVIDENCE, THE GREATEST EVIL OF ALL?
OR IS HOPE TRULY GOOD? HOPE IS GOOD, BUT IT REMAINS IMPRISONED, STILL, IN PANDORA'S JAR?
POOR PROMETHEUS, BOUND BEFORE ME. YOUR BELOVED HUMANKIND STILL SUFFERING UNDER THOSE EVILS.
STILL SUFFERING UNDER THAT BLIND HOPE. HASN'T THAT PUNISHED YOU ENOUGH ALREADY?
YOU HAVE THE GIFT OF FORESIGHT, PROMETHEUS. YOU KNOW WHAT'S COMING FOR YOU.
YOU CLAIM TO KNOW THE DOWNFALL OF ZEUS. TELL ME, AND YOU CAN GO FREE.
I'D RATHER SPEND ALL ETERNITY CHAINED TO THIS ROCK THAN SPEND ONE DAY AS A SERVANT TO ZEUS, LIKE YOU.
YOUR CHOICE, MAN.
HEPHAISTOS! WE DONE HERE?
...AYE.

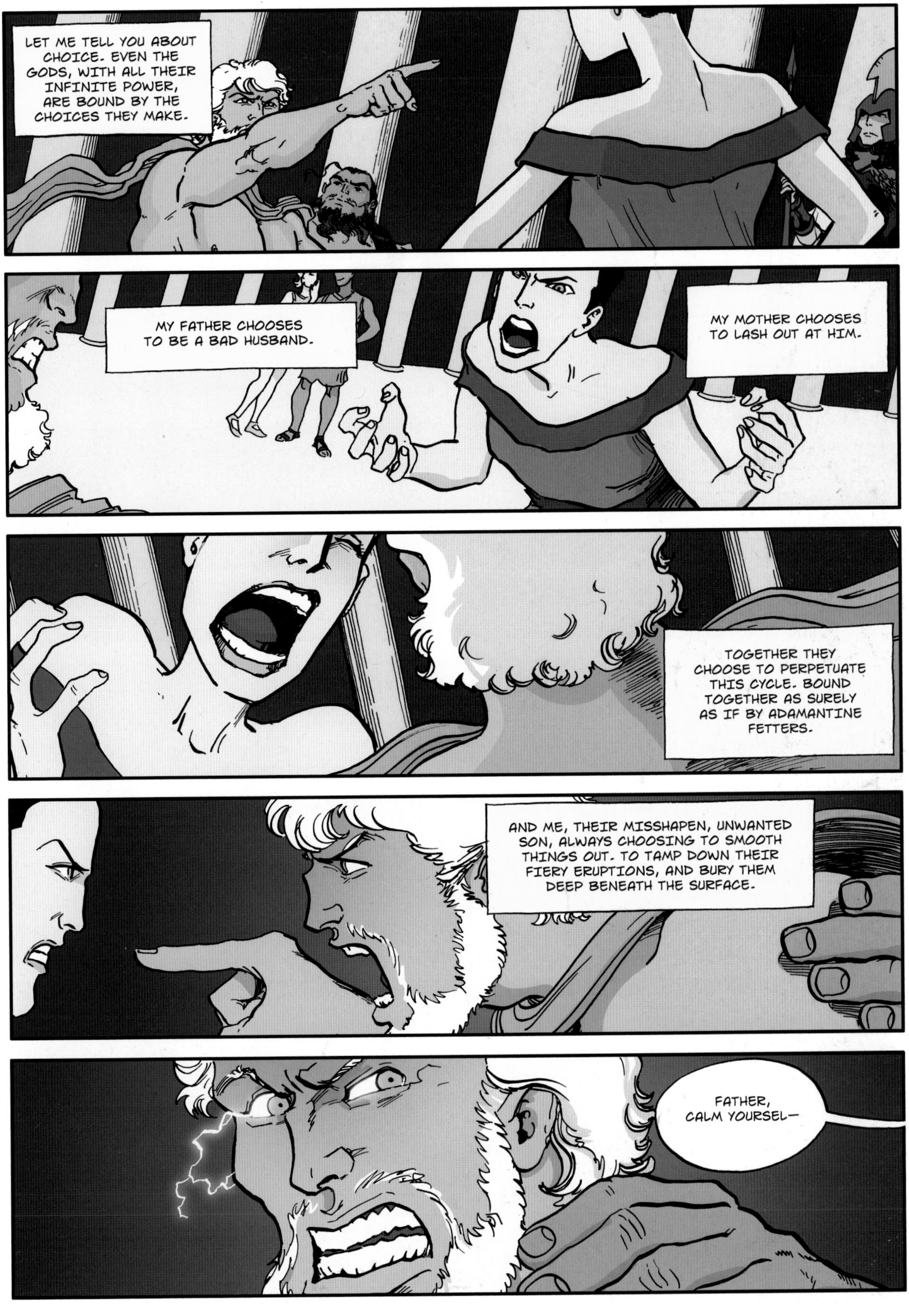
LET ME TELL YOU ABOUT CHOICE. EVEN THE GODS, WITH ALL THEIR INFINITE POWER, ARE BOUND BY THE CHOICES THEY MAKE.
MY FATHER CHOOSES TO BE A BAD HUSBAND.
MY MOTHER CHOOSES TO LASH OUT AT HIM.
TOGETHER THEY CHOOSE TO PERPETUATE THIS CYCLE. BOUND TOGETHER AS SURELY AS IF BY ADAMANTINE FETTERS.
AND ME, THEIR MISSHAPEN, UNWANTED SON, ALWAYS CHOOSING TO SMOOTH THINGS OUT. TO TAMP DOWN THEIR FIERY ERUPTIONS, AND BURY THEM DEEP BENEATH THE SURFACE.
FATHER, CALM YOURSEL—

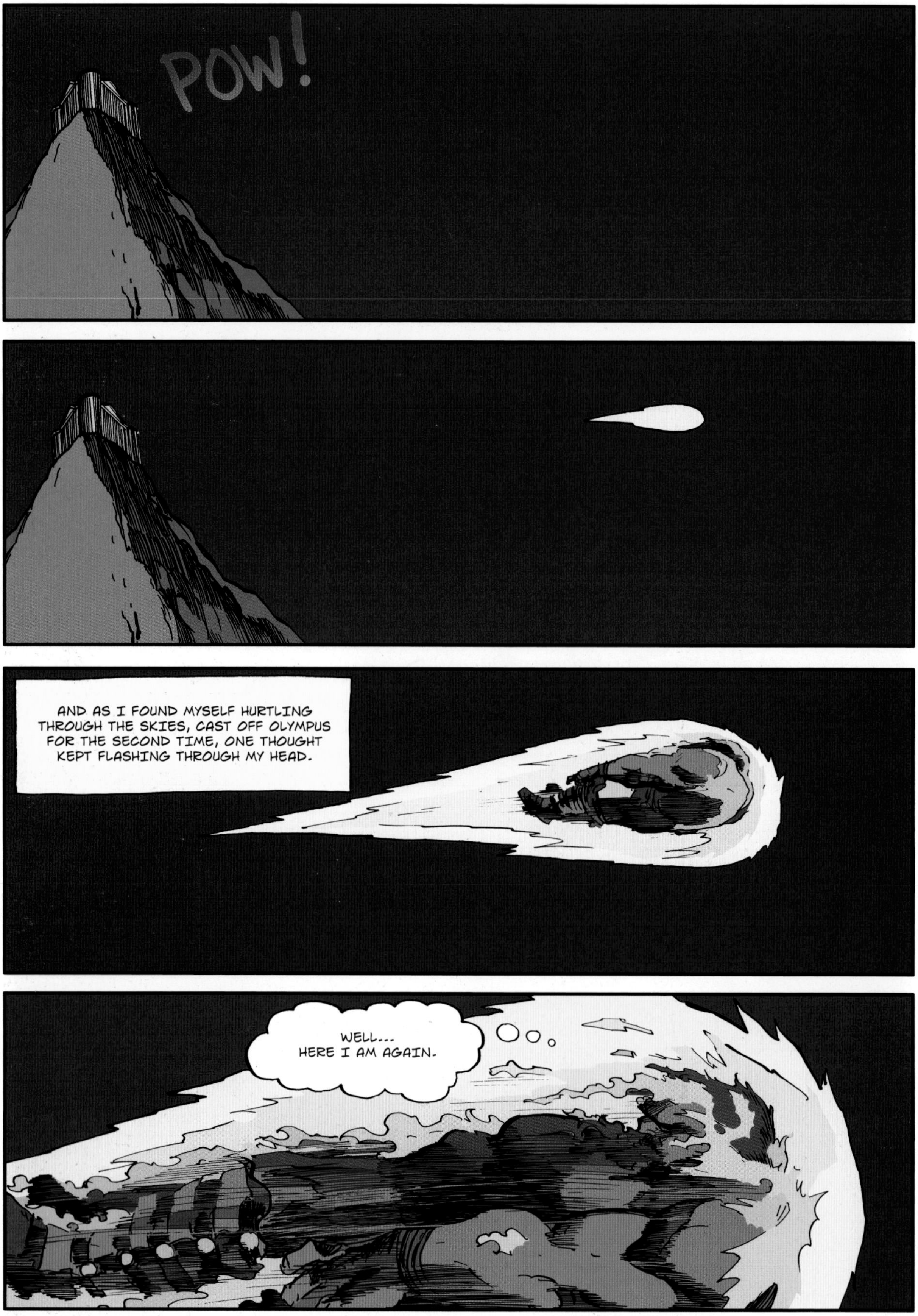
POW!
AND AS I FOUND MYSELF HURTLING THROUGH THE SKIES, CAST OFF OLYMPUS FOR THE SECOND TIME, ONE THOUGHT KEPT FLASHING THROUGH MY HEAD.
WELL... HERE I AM AGAIN.

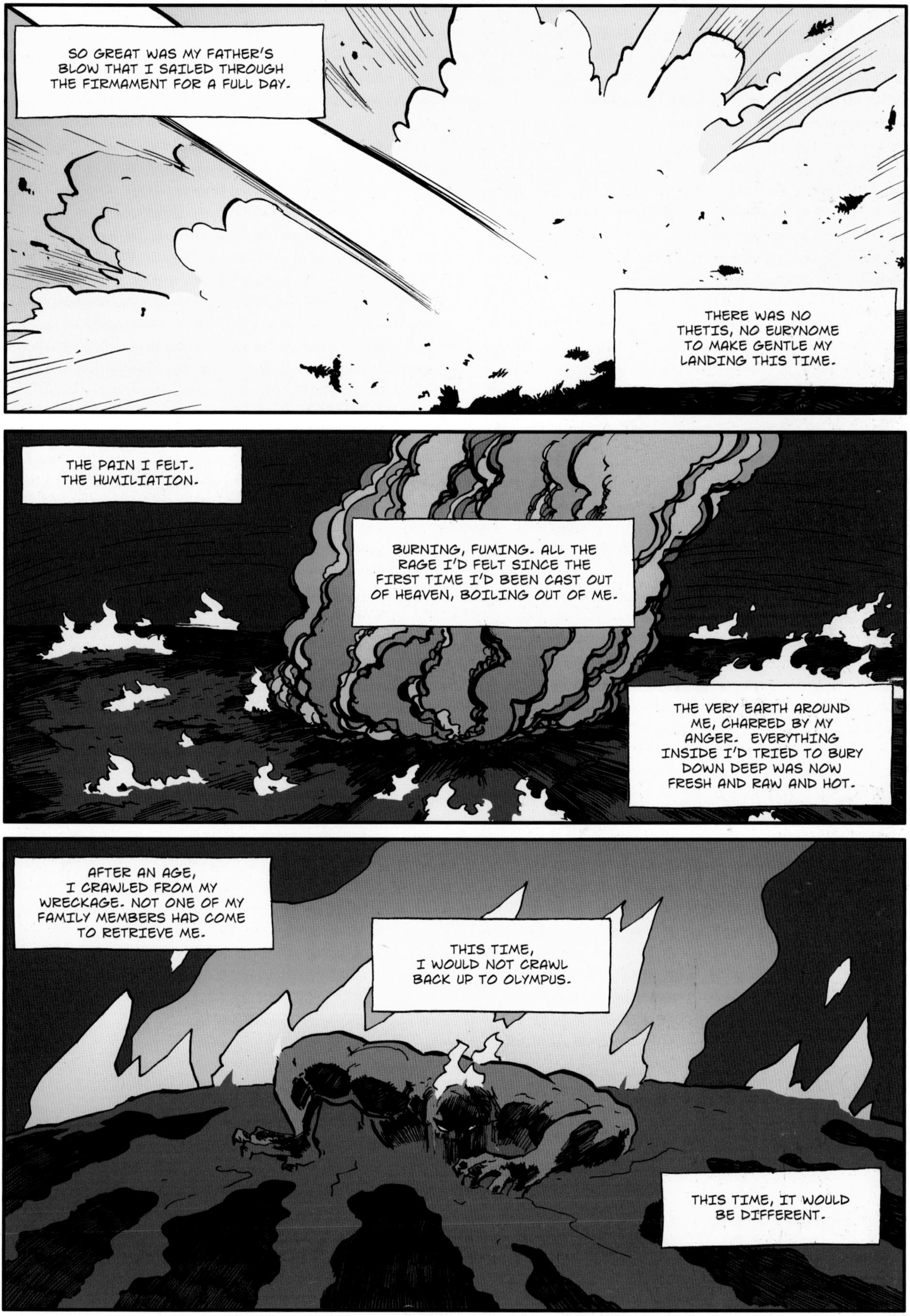
SO GREAT WAS MY FATHER'S BLOW THAT I SAILED THROUGH THE FIRMAMENT FOR A FULL DAY.
THERE WAS NO THETIS, NO EURYNOME TO MAKE GENTLE MY LANDING THIS TIME.
THE PAIN I FELT. THE HUMILIATION.
BURNING, FUMING. ALL THE RAGE I'D FELT SINCE THE FIRST TIME I'D BEEN CAST OUT OF HEAVEN, BOILING OUT OF ME.
THE VERY EARTH AROUND ME, CHARRED BY MY ANGER. EVERYTHING INSIDE I'D TRIED TO BURY DOWN DEEP WAS NOW FRESH AND RAW AND HOT.
AFTER AN AGE, I CRAWLED FROM MY WRECKAGE. NOT ONE OF MY FAMILY MEMBERS HAD COME TO RETRIEVE ME.
THIS TIME, I WOULD NOT CRAWL BACK UP TO OLYMPUS.
THIS TIME, IT WOULD BE DIFFERENT.

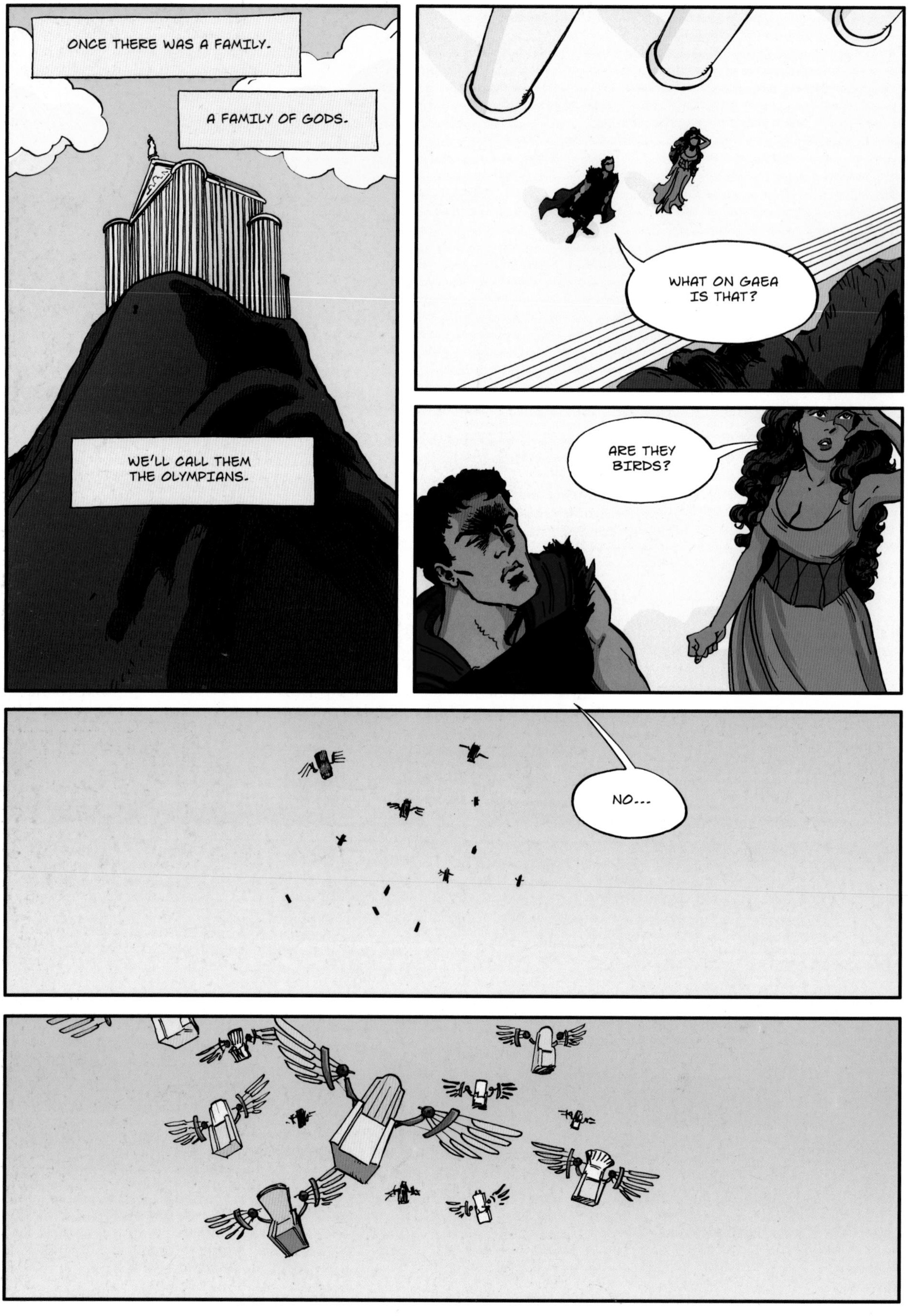
ONCE THERE WAS A FAMILY.
A FAMILY OF GODS.
WE'LL CALL THEM THE OLYMPIANS.
WHAT ON GAEA IS THAT?
ARE THEY BIRDS?
NO...

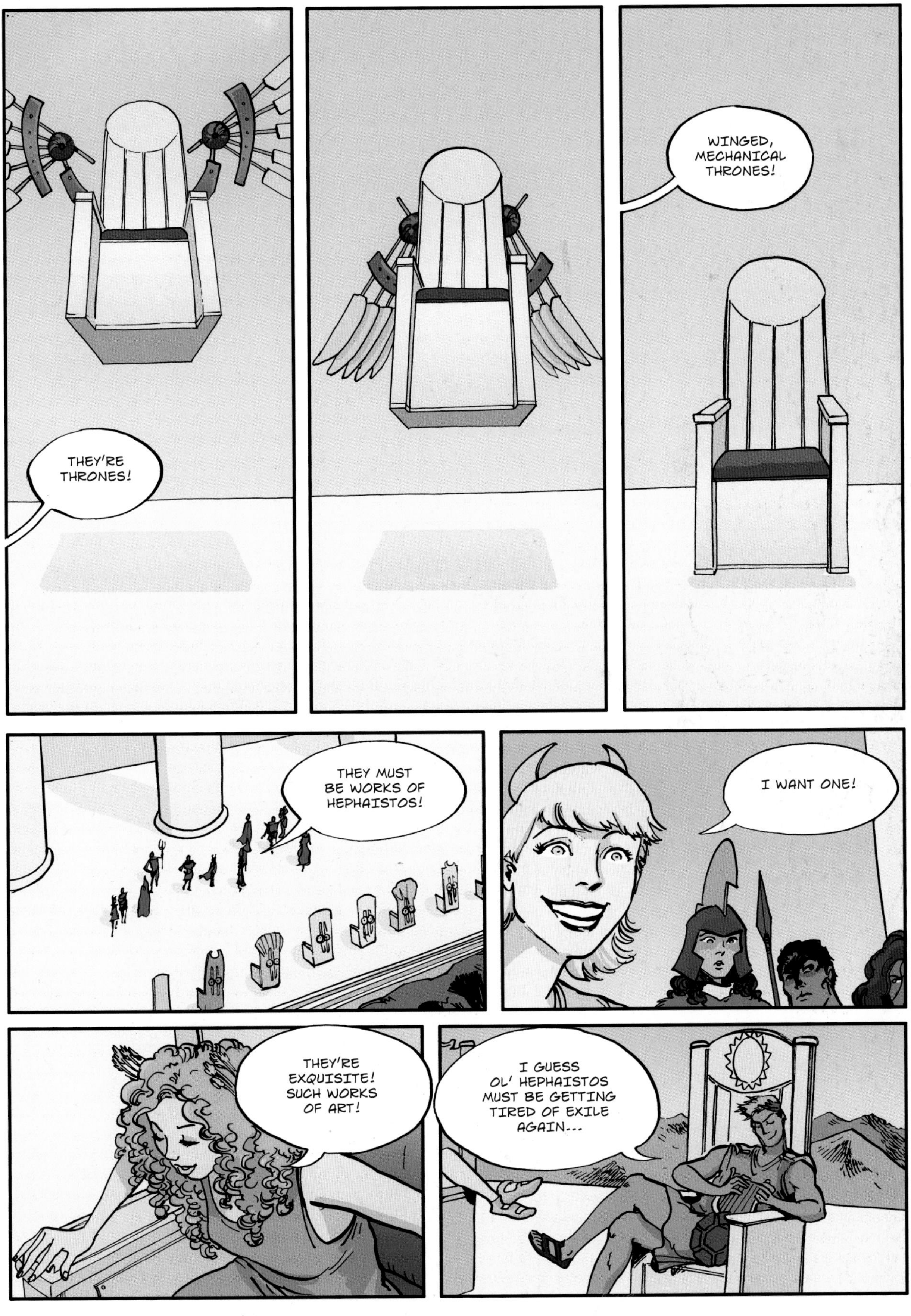
THEY'RE THRONES!
WINGED, MECHANICAL THRONES!
THEY MUST BE WORKS OF HEPHAISTOS!
I WANT ONE!
THEY'RE EXQUISITE! SUCH WORKS OF ART!
I GUESS OL' HEPHAISTOS MUST BE GETTING TIRED OF EXILE AGAIN...

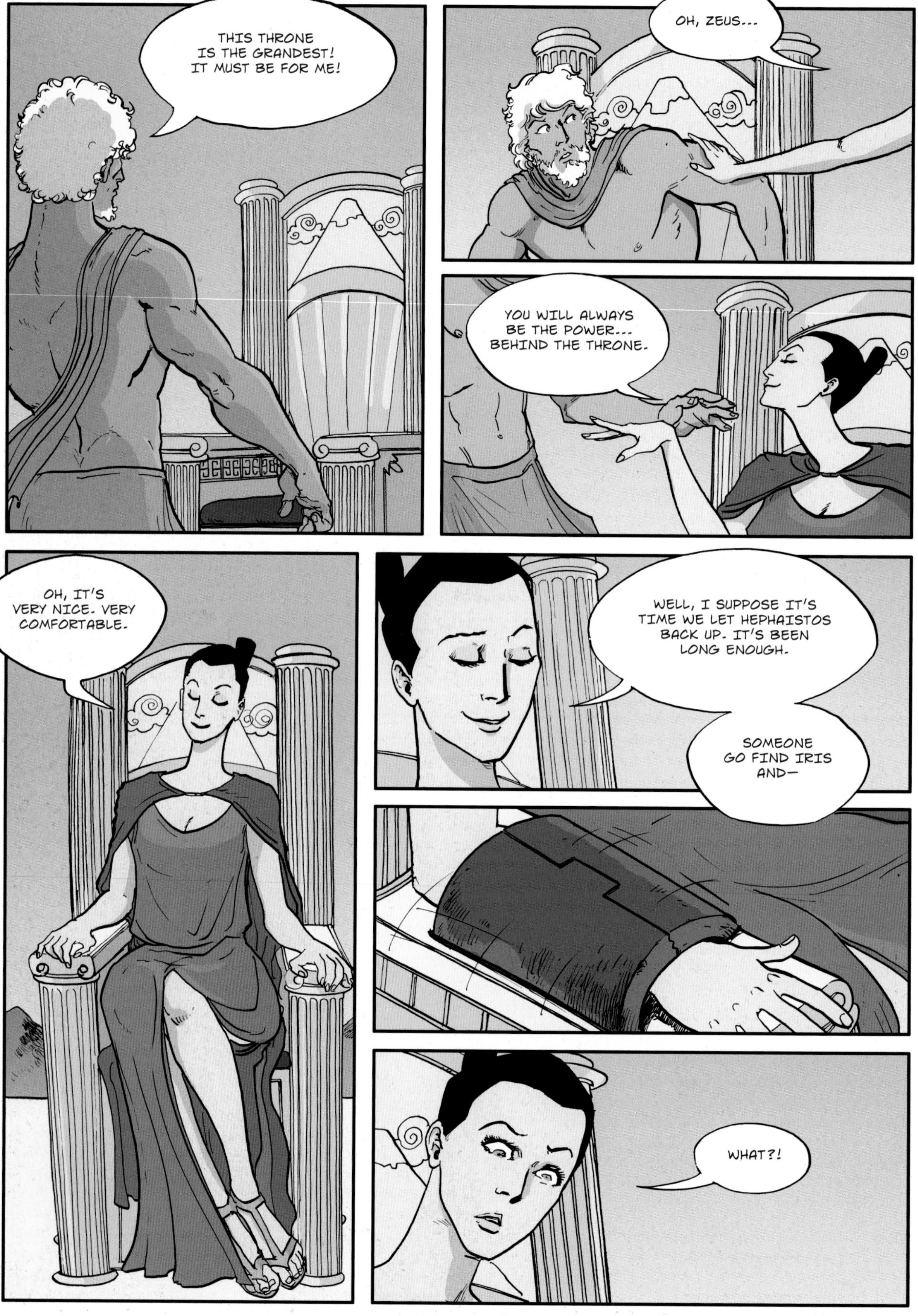
THIS THRONE IS THE GRANDEST! IT MUST BE FOR ME!
OH, ZEUS...
YOU WILL ALWAYS BE THE POWER... BEHIND THE THRONE.
OH, IT'S VERY NICE. VERY COMFORTABLE.
WELL, I SUPPOSE IT'S TIME WE LET HEPHAISTOS BACK UP. IT'S BEEN LONG ENOUGH.
SOMEONE GO FIND IRIS AND—
WHAT?!

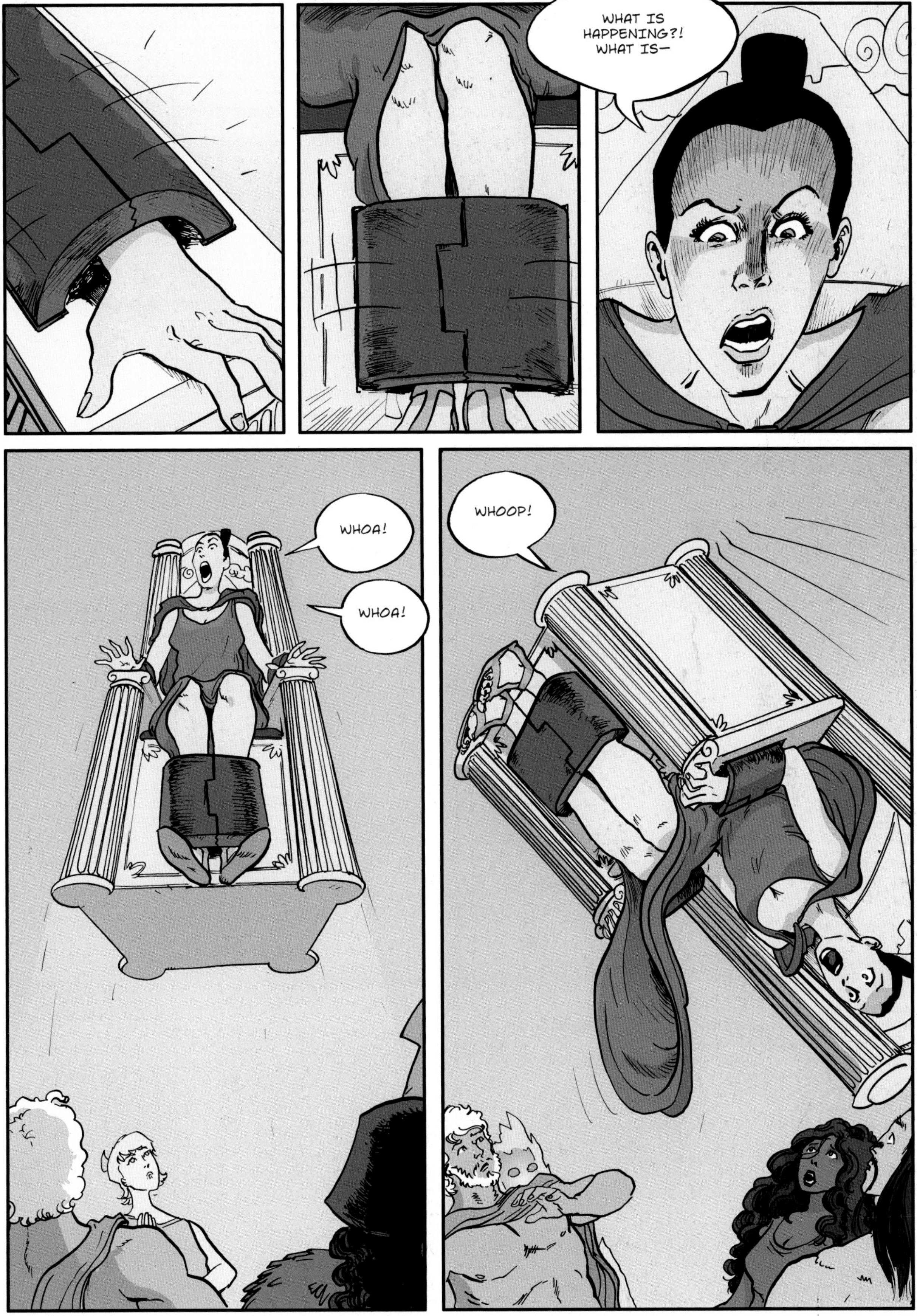

WHAT IS HAPPENING?! WHAT IS—
WHOA!
WHOA!
WHOOP!

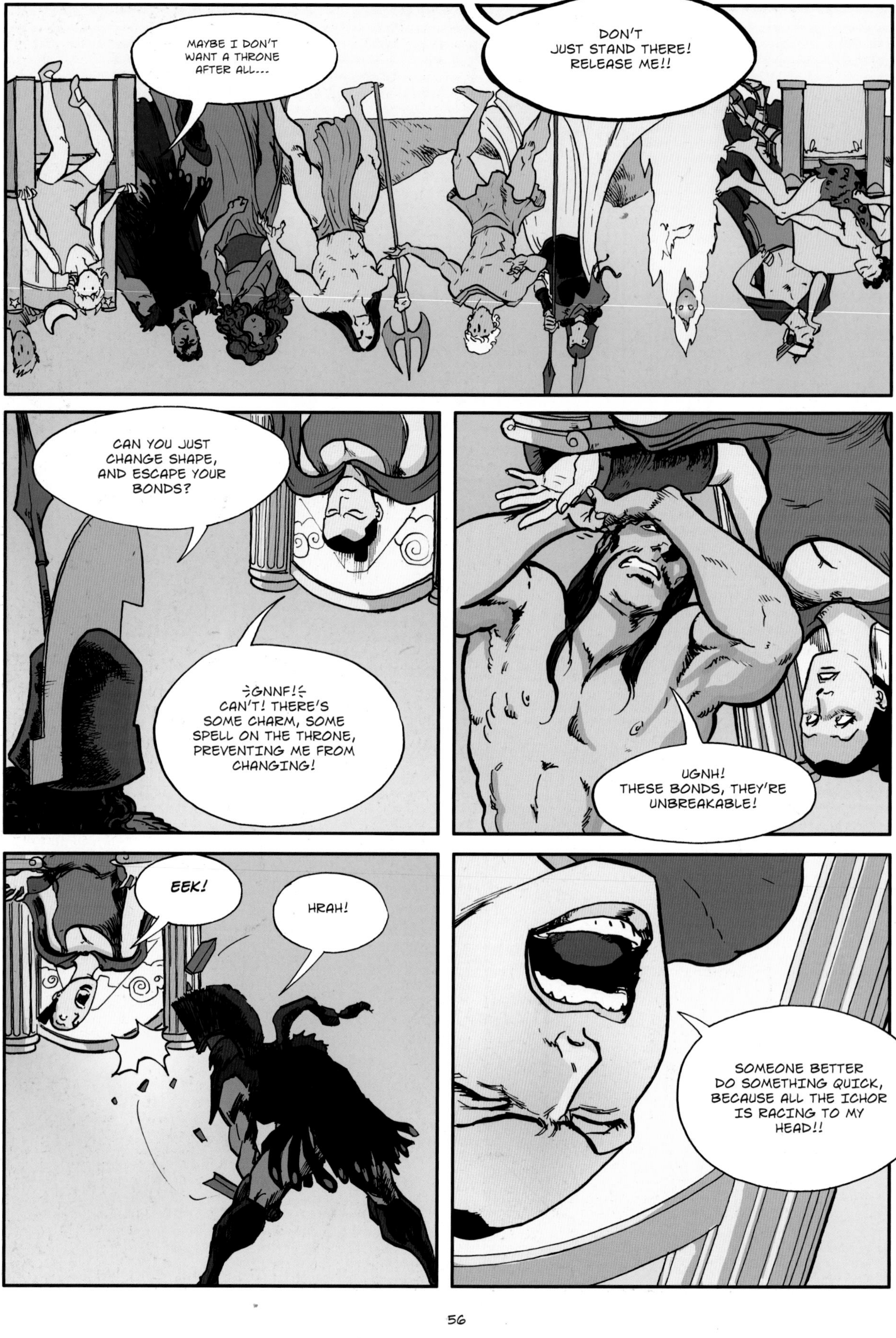
MAYBE I DON'T WANT A THRONE AFTER ALL...
DON'T JUST STAND THERE! RELEASE ME!!
CAN YOU JUST CHANGE SHAPE, AND ESCAPE YOUR BONDS?
GNNF! CAN'T! THERE'S SOME CHARM, SOME SPELL ON THE THRONE, PREVENTING ME FROM CHANGING!
UGNH! THESE BONDS, THEY'RE UNBREAKABLE!
EEK!
HRAH!
SOMEONE BETTER DO SOMETHING QUICK, BECAUSE ALL THE ICHOR IS RACING TO MY HEAD!!

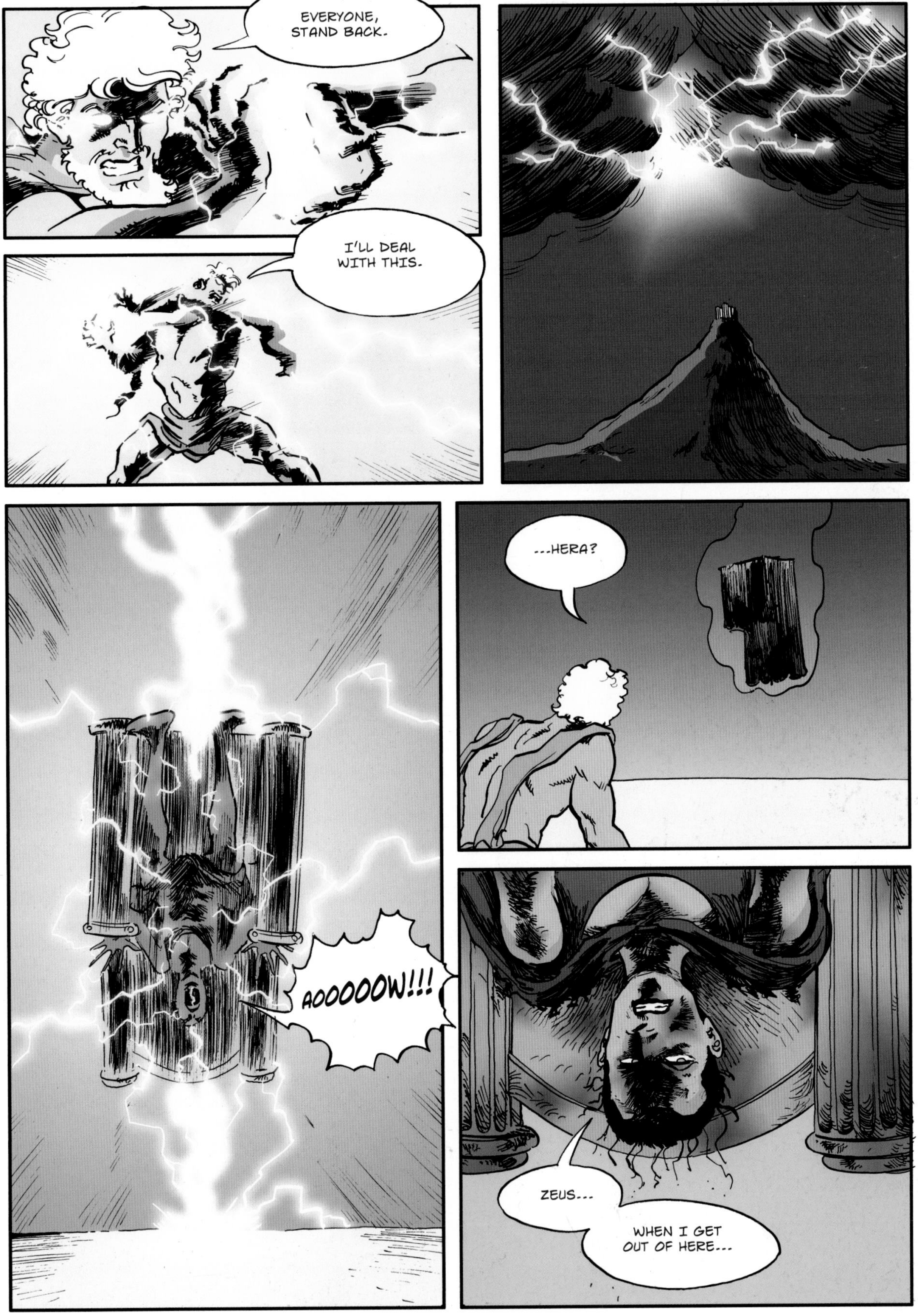
EVERYONE, STAND BACK.
I'LL DEAL WITH THIS.
...HERA?
AOOOOOW!!!
ZEUS...
WHEN I GET OUT OF HERE...

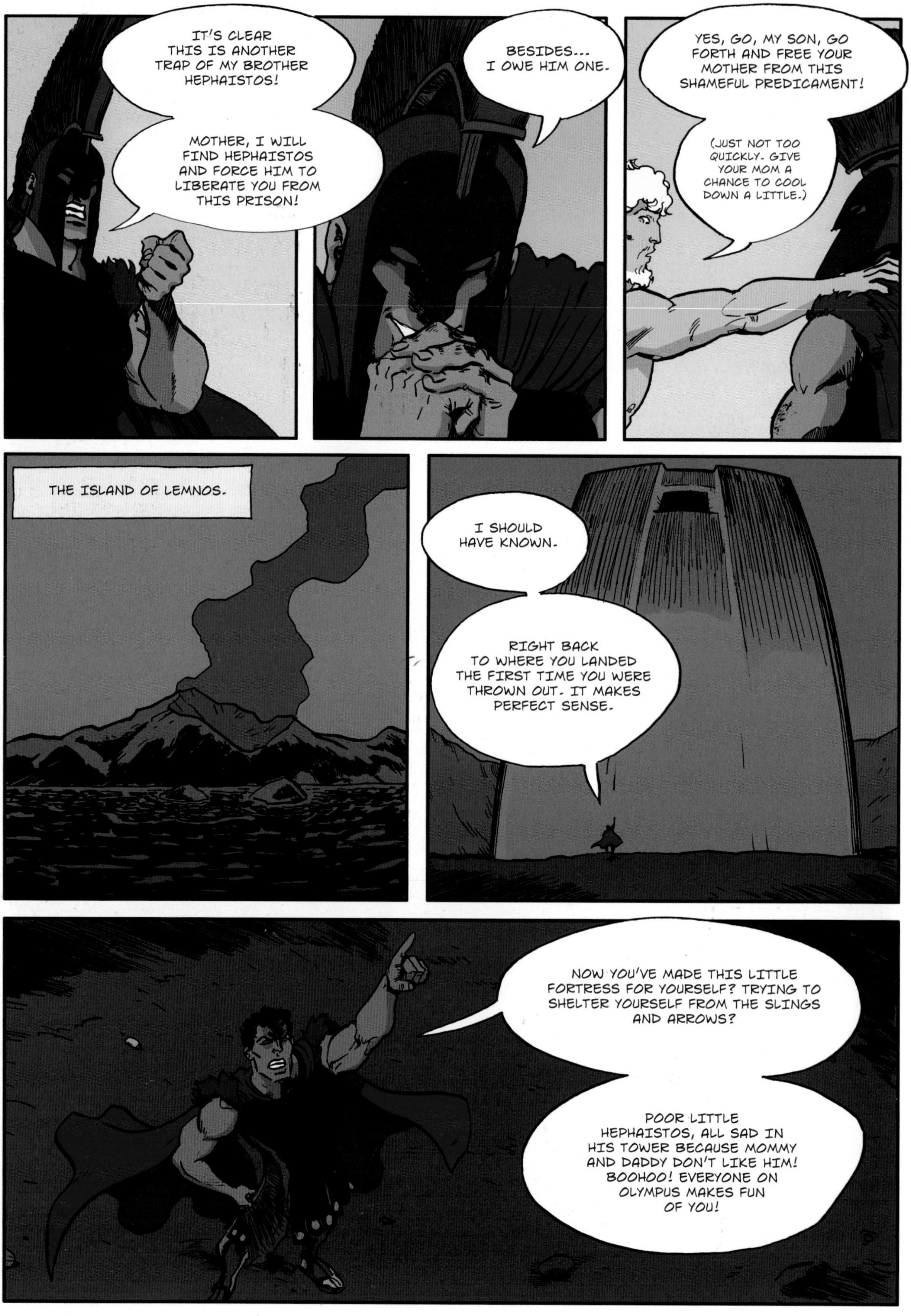
IT'S CLEAR THIS IS ANOTHER TRAP OF MY BROTHER HEPHAISTOS!
MOTHER, I WILL FIND HEPHAISTOS AND FORCE HIM TO LIBERATE YOU FROM THIS PRISON!
BESIDES... I OWE HIM ONE.
YES, GO, MY SON, GO FORTH AND FREE YOUR MOTHER FROM THIS SHAMEFUL PREDICAMENT!
(JUST NOT TOO QUICKLY. GIVE YOUR MOM A CHANCE TO COOL DOWN A LITTLE.)
THE ISLAND OF LEMNOS.
I SHOULD HAVE KNOWN.
RIGHT BACK TO WHERE YOU LANDED THE FIRST TIME YOU WERE THROWN OUT. IT MAKES PERFECT SENSE.
NOW YOU'VE MADE THIS LITTLE FORTRESS FOR YOURSELF? TRYING TO SHELTER YOURSELF FROM THE SLINGS AND ARROWS?
POOR LITTLE HEPHAISTOS, ALL SAD IN HIS TOWER BECAUSE MOMMY AND DADDY DON'T LIKE HIM! BOOHOO! EVERYONE ON OLYMPUS MAKES FUN OF YOU!

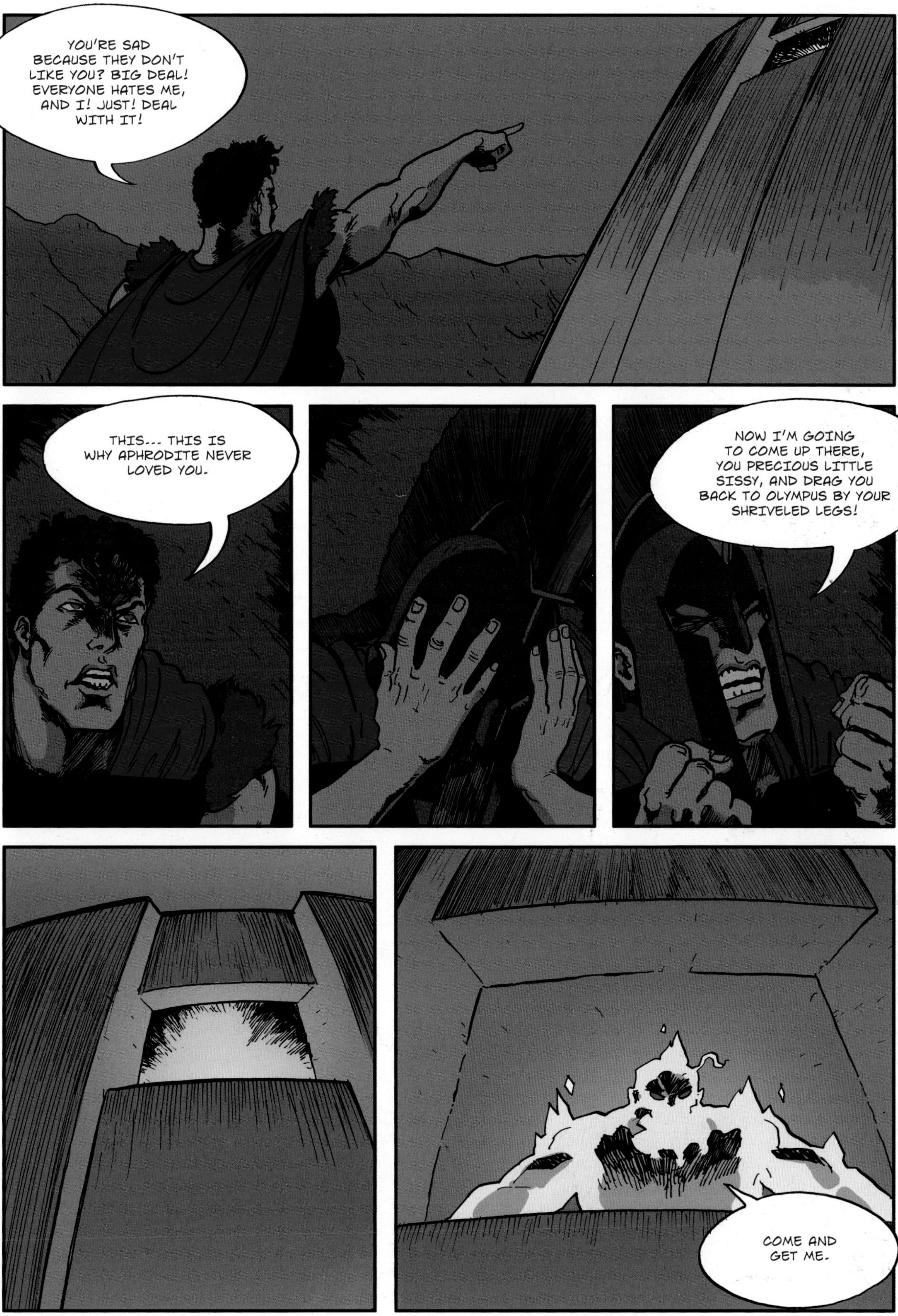
YOU'RE SAD BECAUSE THEY DON'T LIKE YOU? BIG DEAL! EVERYONE HATES ME, AND I! JUST! DEAL WITH IT!
THIS... THIS IS WHY APHRODITE NEVER LOVED YOU.
NOW I'M GOING TO COME UP THERE, YOU PRECIOUS LITTLE SISSY, AND DRAG YOU BACK TO OLYMPUS BY YOUR SHRIVELED LEGS!
COME AND GET ME.

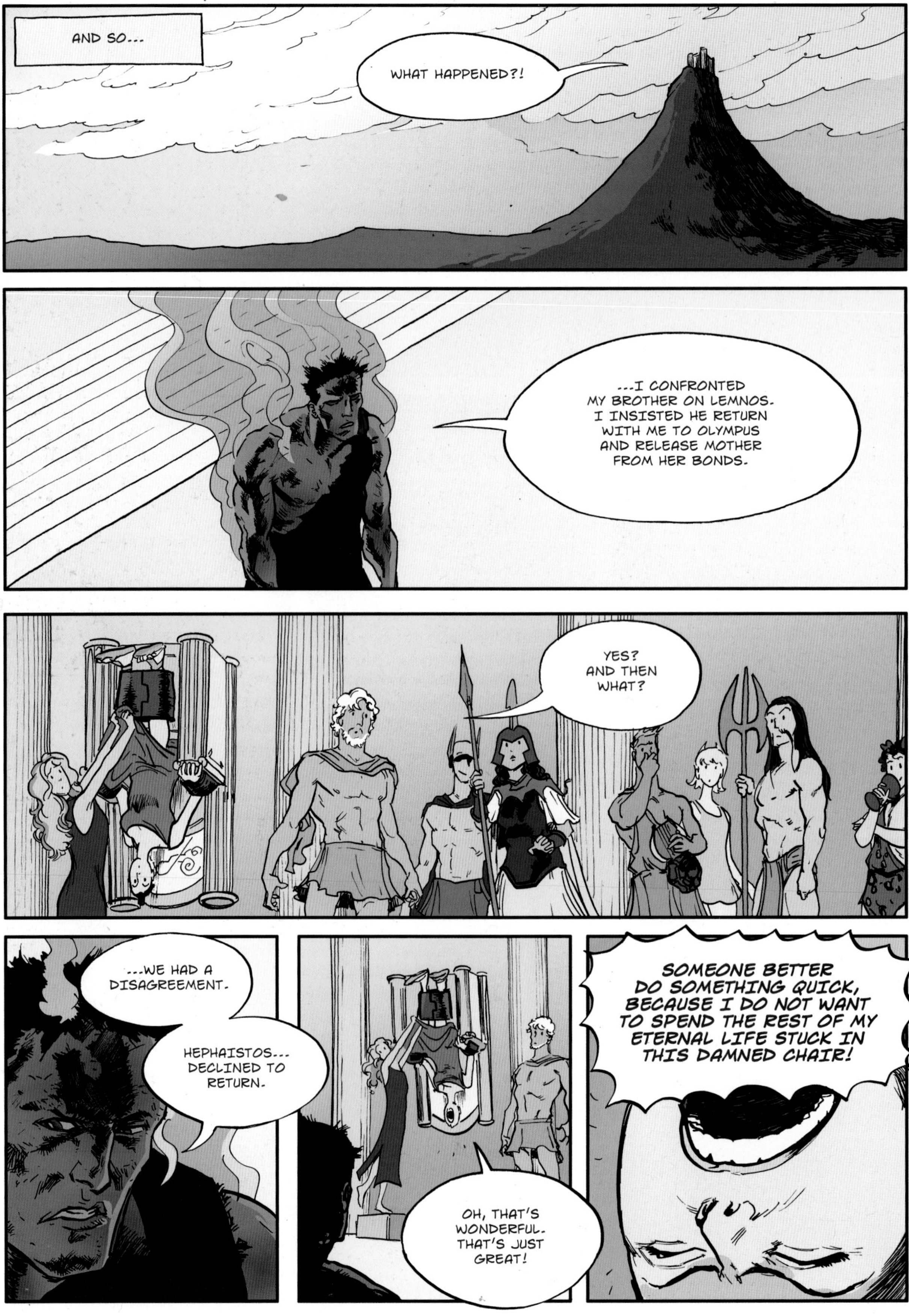

AND SO...
WHAT HAPPENED?!
...I CONFRONTED MY BROTHER ON LEMNOS. I INSISTED HE RETURN WITH ME TO OLYMPUS AND RELEASE MOTHER FROM HER BONDS.
YES? AND THEN WHAT?
...WE HAD A DISAGREEMENT.
HEPHAISTOS... DECLINED TO RETURN.
OH, THAT'S WONDERFUL. THAT'S JUST GREAT!
SOMEONE BETTER DO SOMETHING QUICK, BECAUSE I DO NOT WANT TO SPEND THE REST OF MY ETERNAL LIFE STUCK IN THIS DAMNED CHAIR!

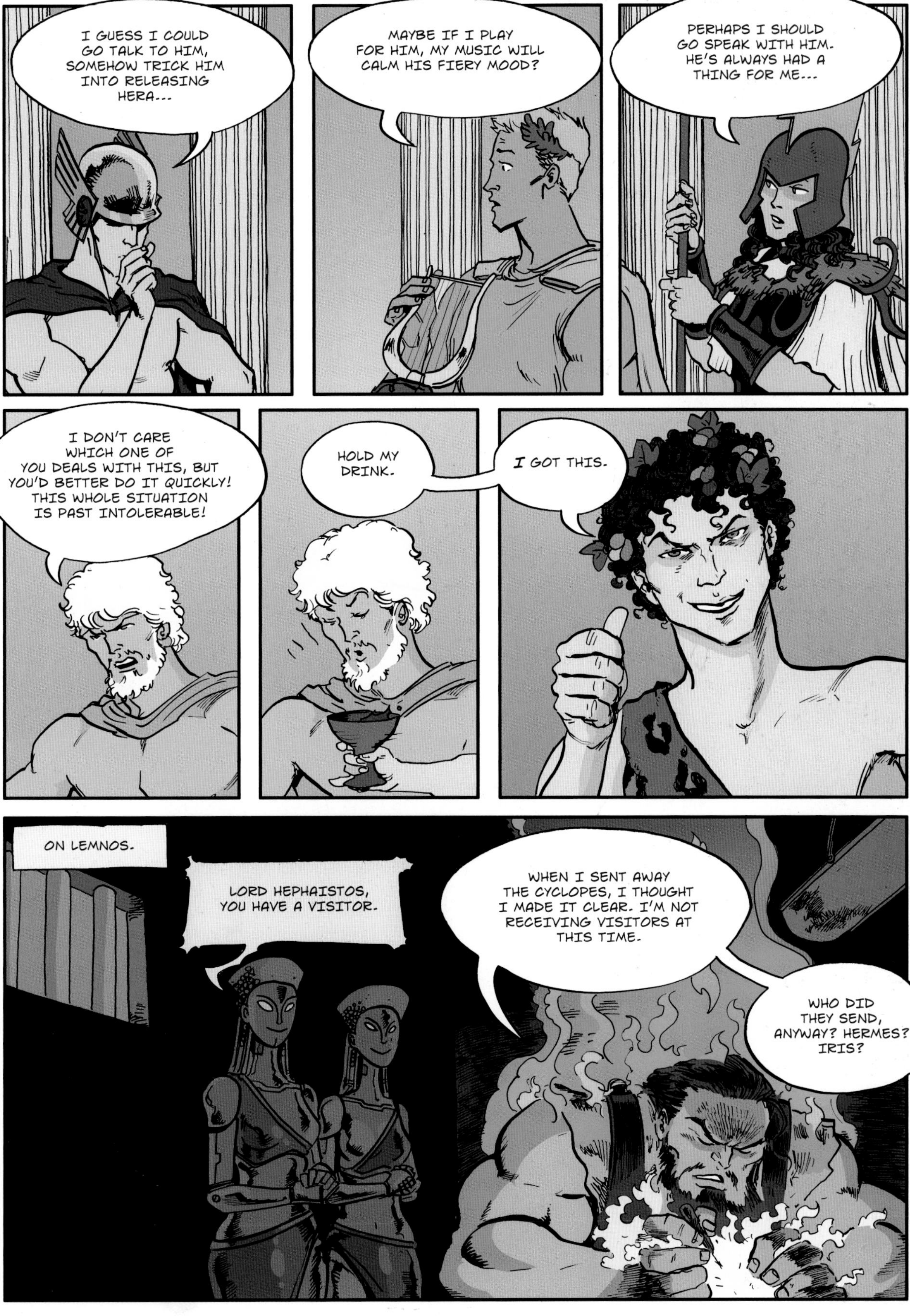
I GUESS I COULD GO TALK TO HIM, SOMEHOW TRICK HIM INTO RELEASING HERA...
MAYBE IF I PLAY FOR HIM, MY MUSIC WILL CALM HIS FIERY MOOD?
PERHAPS I SHOULD GO SPEAK WITH HIM. HE'S ALWAYS HAD A THING FOR ME...
I DON'T CARE WHICH ONE OF YOU DEALS WITH THIS, BUT YOU'D BETTER DO IT QUICKLY! THIS WHOLE SITUATION IS PAST INTOLERABLE!
HOLD MY DRINK.
I GOT THIS.
ON LEMNOS.
LORD HEPHAISTOS, YOU HAVE A VISITOR.
WHEN I SENT AWAY THE CYCLOPES, I THOUGHT I MADE IT CLEAR. I'M NOT RECEIVING VISITORS AT THIS TIME.
WHO DID THEY SEND, ANYWAY? HERMES? IRIS?

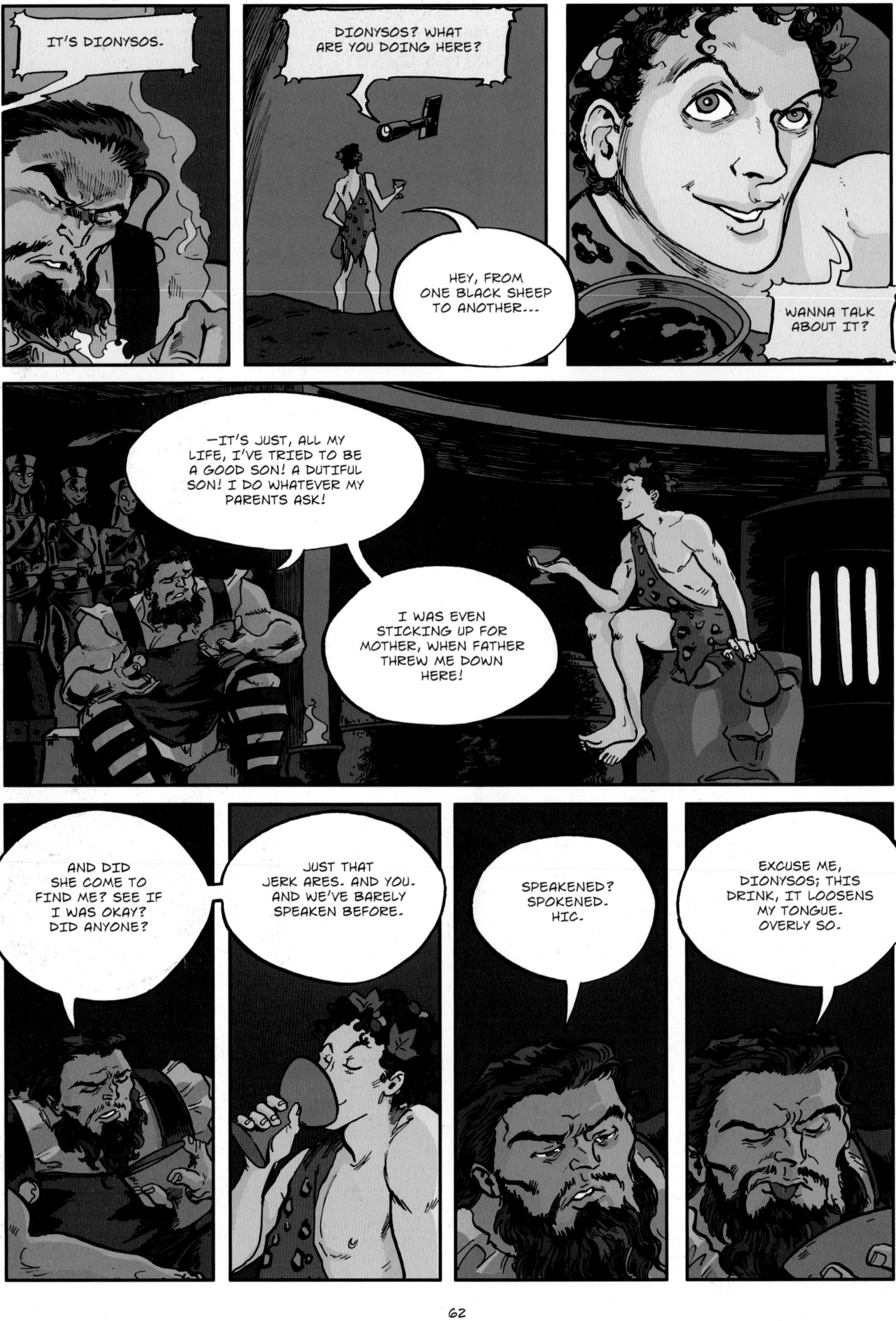
IT'S DIONYSOS.
DIONYSOS? WHAT ARE YOU DOING HERE?
HEY, FROM ONE BLACK SHEEP TO ANOTHER...
WANNA TALK ABOUT IT?
—IT'S JUST, ALL MY LIFE, I'VE TRIED TO BE A GOOD SON! A DUTIFUL SON! I DO WHATEVER MY PARENTS ASK!
I WAS EVEN STICKING UP FOR MOTHER, WHEN FATHER THREW ME DOWN HERE!
AND DID SHE COME TO FIND ME? SEE IF I WAS OKAY? DID ANYONE?
JUST THAT JERK ARES. AND YOU. AND WE'VE BARELY SPEAKEN BEFORE.
SPEAKENED? SPOKENED. HIC.
EXCUSE ME, DIONYSOS; THIS DRINK, IT LOOSENS MY TONGUE. OVERLY SO.

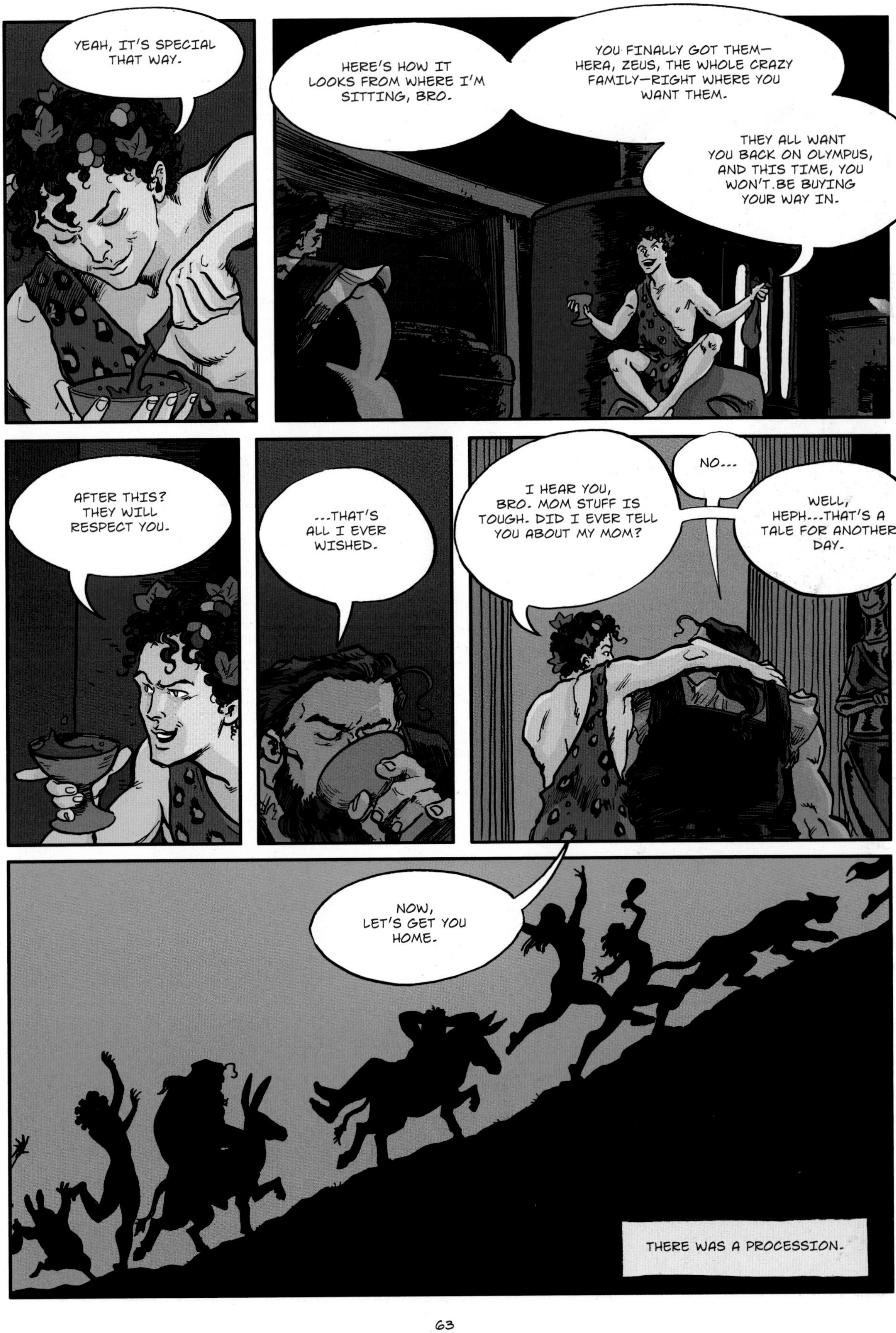
YEAH, IT'S SPECIAL THAT WAY.
HERE'S HOW IT LOOKS FROM WHERE I'M SITTING, BRO.
YOU FINALLY GOT THEM—HERA, ZEUS, THE WHOLE CRAZY FAMILY—RIGHT WHERE YOU WANT THEM.
THEY ALL WANT YOU BACK ON OLYMPUS, AND THIS TIME, YOU WON'T BE BUYING YOUR WAY IN.
AFTER THIS? THEY WILL RESPECT YOU.
...THAT'S ALL I EVER WISHED.
I HEAR YOU, BRO. MOM STUFF IS TOUGH. DID I EVER TELL YOU ABOUT MY MOM?
NO...
WELL, HEPH...THAT'S A TALE FOR ANOTHER DAY.
NOW, LET'S GET YOU HOME.
THERE WAS A PROCESSION.

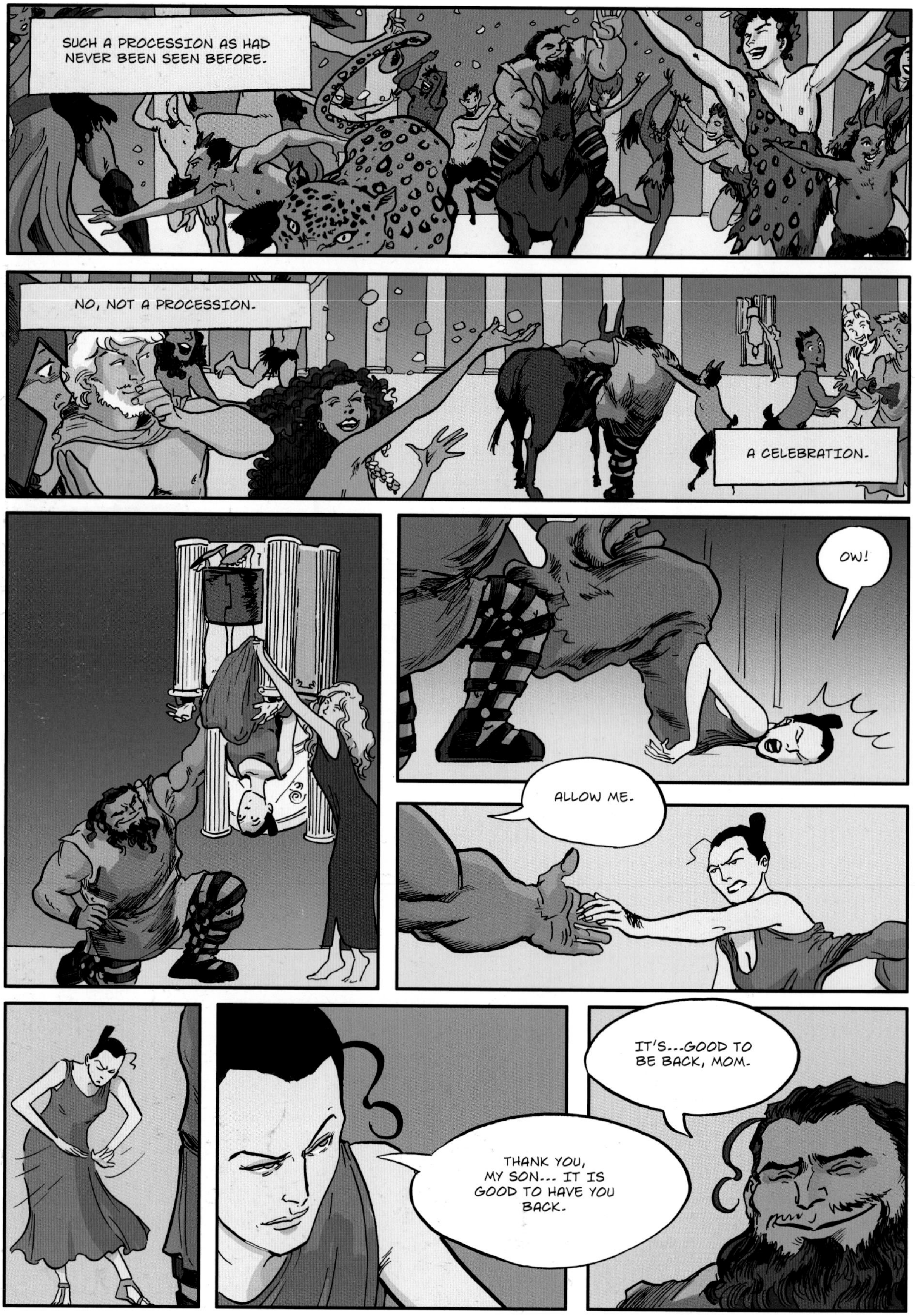
SUCH A PROCESSION AS HAD NEVER BEEN SEEN BEFORE.
NO, NOT A PROCESSION.
A CELEBRATION.
OW!
ALLOW ME.
THANK YOU, MY SON... IT IS GOOD TO HAVE YOU BACK.
IT'S...GOOD TO BE BACK, MOM.

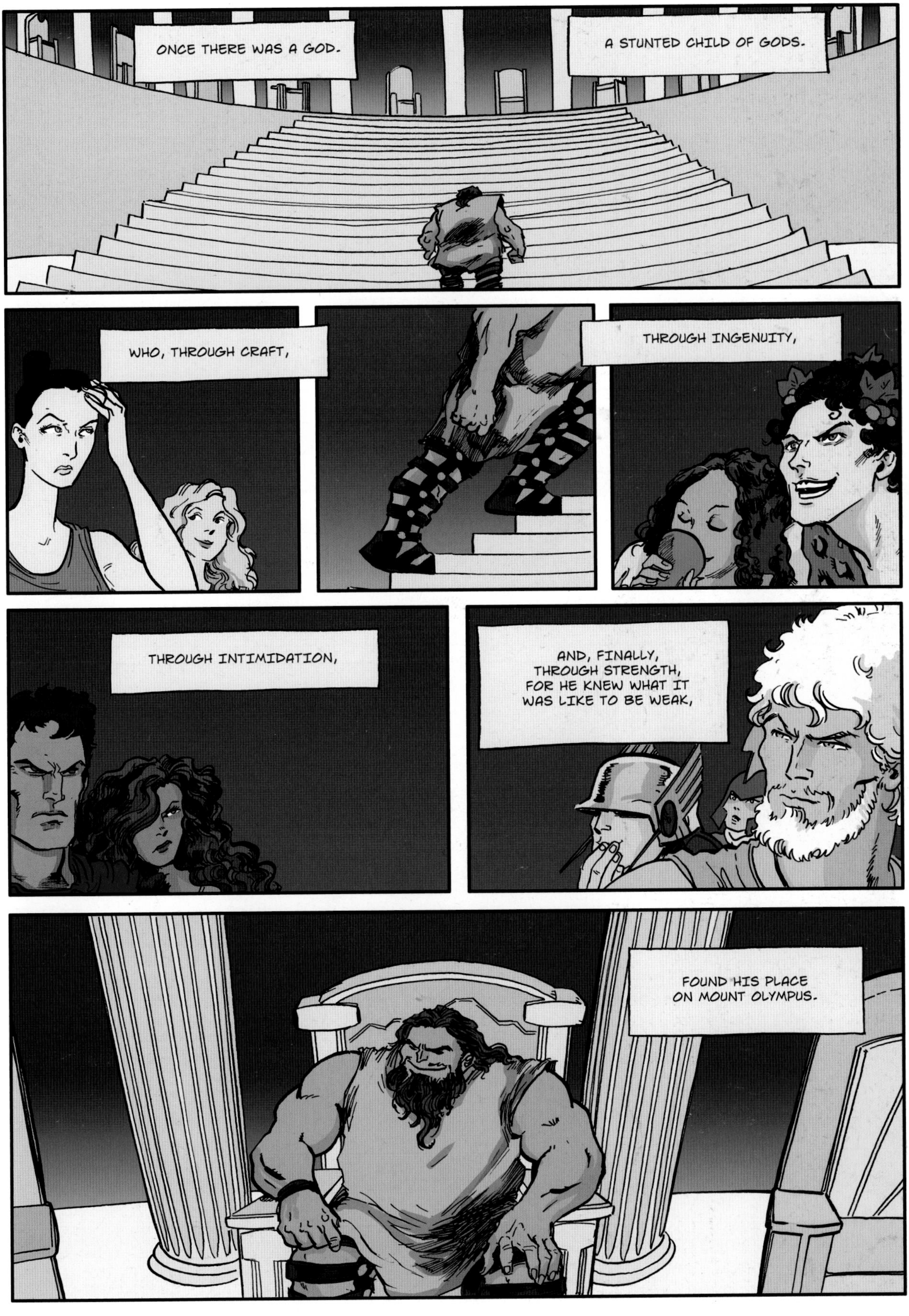
ONCE THERE WAS A GOD.
A STUNTED CHILD OF GODS.
WHO, THROUGH CRAFT,
THROUGH INGENUITY,
THROUGH INTIMIDATION,
AND, FINALLY, THROUGH STRENGTH, FOR HE KNEW WHAT IT WAS LIKE TO BE WEAK,
FOUND HIS PLACE ON MOUNT OLYMPUS.

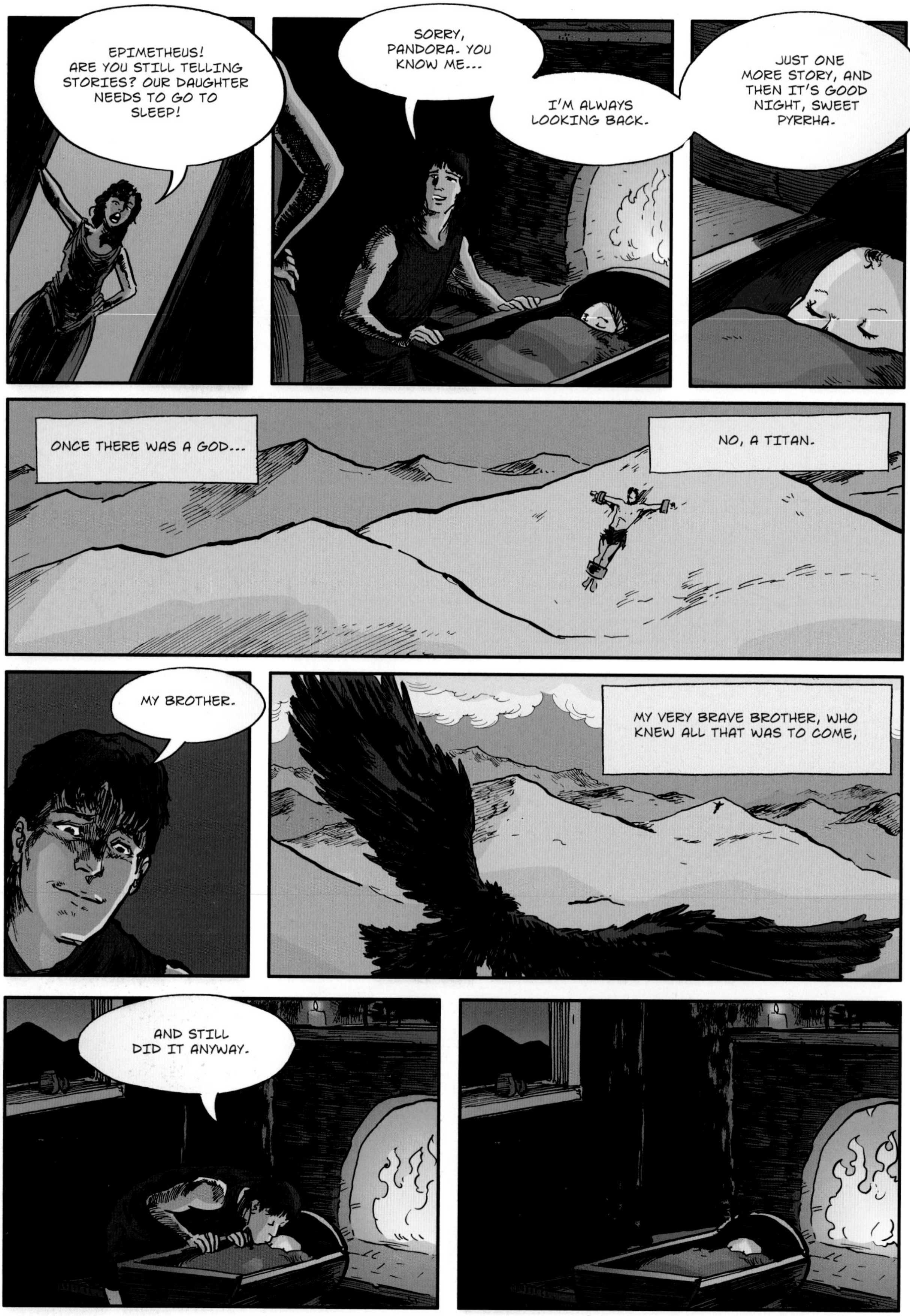
EPIMETHEUS! ARE YOU STILL TELLING STORIES? OUR DAUGHTER NEEDS TO GO TO SLEEP!
SORRY, PANDORA. YOU KNOW ME...
I'M ALWAYS LOOKING BACK.
JUST ONE MORE STORY, AND THEN IT'S GOOD NIGHT, SWEET PYRRHA.
ONCE THERE WAS A GOD...
NO, A TITAN.
MY BROTHER.
MY VERY BRAVE BROTHER, WHO KNEW ALL THAT WAS TO COME,
AND STILL DID IT ANYWAY.

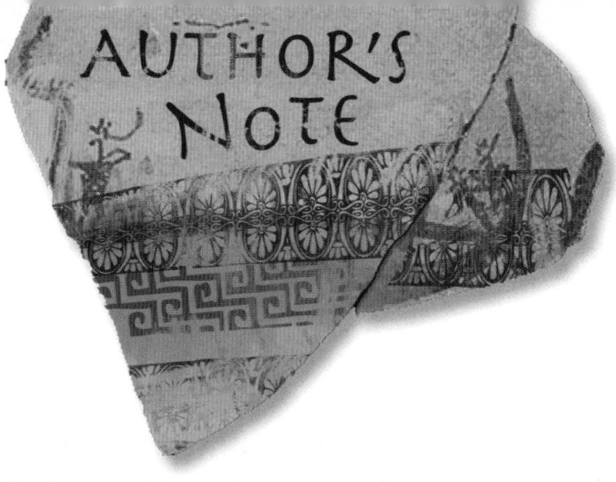
AUTHOR'S NOTE

I've been working on OLYMPIANS for a pretty long time now.

Roughly ten years, by my reckoning. About as long as it took Odysseus to return home after the Trojan War. Maybe even as long as the Titanomachy, the clash between the gods and the Titans. That's probably longer than a lot of my readers have even been alive.

As I near the completion of this series, I find it interesting to see how much my vision of it has changed. Not just in the art, though that is worth mentioning—for a decade now, I've been drawing the adventures of fantastically beautiful gods and goddesses. It was a welcome change to get grimy and gritty and chronicle the adventures of ugly ol' Hephaistos (although he's really not that ugly, is he, folks?). No, my vision of the series has changed in the writing as well.

My initial plan for the book you are holding was that, as Hephaistos was binding him to the Caucasus Mountains, wily Prometheus would subject Hephaistos to a withering armchair-psychology diagnosis. The ugliness of Hephaistos was going to be the crux of this volume—specifically, *why* is Hephaistos ugly? He, like all the Olympians, can assume any form he wants. I was going to reveal, essentially, through the stories I retold and Prometheus's questioning, that Hephaistos basically has bad self-esteem. The guy has had a lot of hard knocks; it would be totally understandable if he did. And that bad self-image, then, is what caused Hephaistos to manifest himself as an ugly man.

Here's the thing, though. You hear writers talk a lot about this: When they are writing characters that they have been writing for a long time, after a while...the characters begin writing themselves. And let me tell you, that is totally true. As much as I tried to wrestle Hephaistos into an unsure and self-pitying role, he refused to bend and yield. Through force and strength, he showed me that while he has been victimized, he does not sit back and take it. Hephaistos is not a shy, withdrawn figure—he returns to Olympus like a boss. He is sweet-tempered and good-natured, but when a line is crossed, he literally erupts like a volcano. Whatever else Hephaistos might suffer from, a poor self-image is not one of his afflictions.

So the question of why Hephaistos manifests himself as an ugly man remains unanswered, at least by this humble scribe, and instead has been ferried off to the "For Discussion" section of this book, where more nimble minds than mine might take a crack at it.

It's been my honor and greatest pleasure to write these books. I'll miss these gods, goddesses, heroes, and monsters, who will have been my constant companions for over a decade once I have finished this series.

But I doubt I'll be missing them forever. After all, they've begun writing themselves...

George O'Connor
Brooklyn, NY
2019

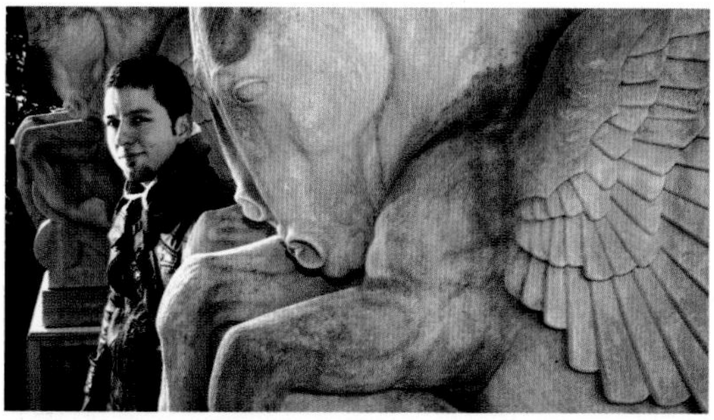

HEPHAISTOS

GOD OF FIRE

GOD OF Fire, Blacksmiths, Craftsmen, Technology, Volcanism

ROMAN NAME Vulcan

SYMBOLS Fire, the Forge, Hammer, Blacksmith Tongs, Axe

SACRED ANIMALS Donkey (his mount on his return to Olympus), Crane, Ox, Oyster (because of their pearls)

SACRED PLACES Lemnos (center of his cult and thought to be the site of his workshop); Mount Etna, Sicily (another site believed to be home to his workshop); Hephaisteion (his temple in Athens—one of the best preserved of all Greek temples)

MONTH September

HEAVENLY BODIES There is a near-Earth asteroid named 2212 Hephaistos. Much more famously, in the Star Trek universe, the character Spock was born on Vulcan (from Hephaistos's Roman name). The inhabitants of this planet are likewise known as Vulcans.

MODERN LEGACY The modern word "volcano" is derived from Hephaistos's Roman name. The ancients believed volcanic eruptions were inadvertently caused by this god as he worked at his forge.

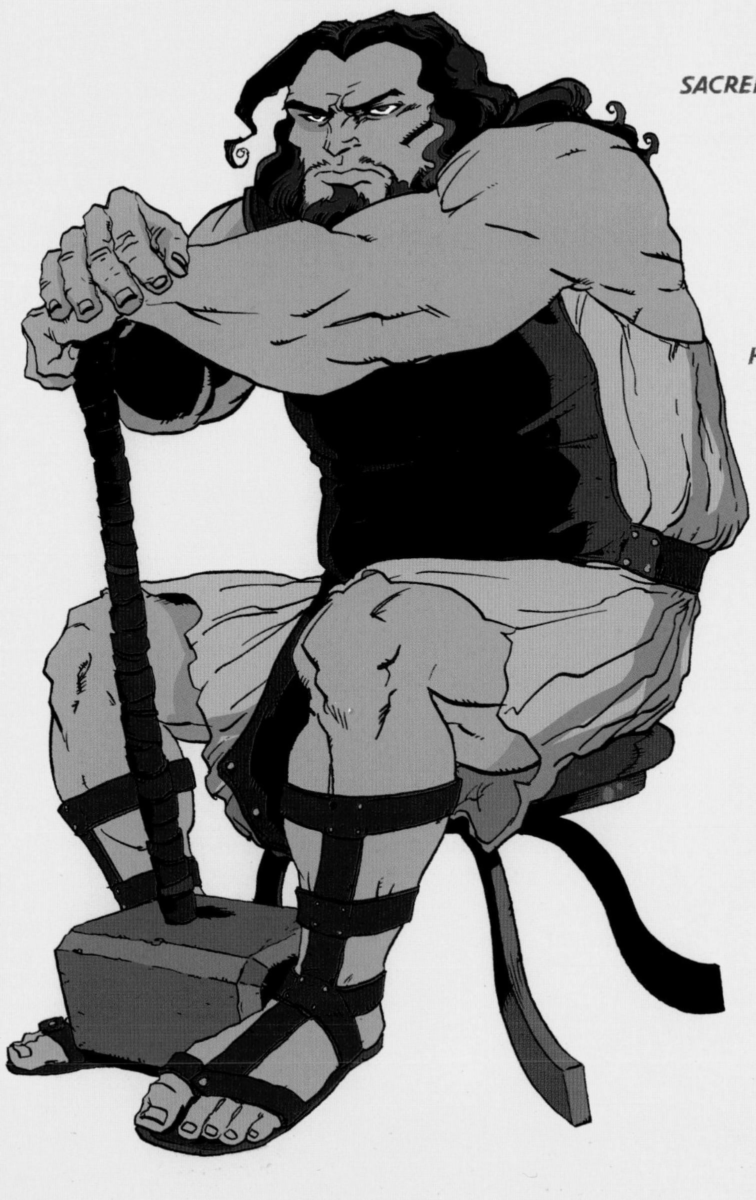

GREEK NOTES

PAGES 2–5: Many of these panels are reworkings of what we read in OLYMPIANS Book 1, *Zeus: King of the Gods*. It was very fun for me to go back and revisit these images and redraw them, and see how much my artistic style has evolved over the course of this series.

PAGE 6: The scenes in this book between Prometheus and Hephaistos are loosely based on *Prometheus Bound*, the ancient Greek tragedy by Aeschylus. If you've read that play or seen it performed, some of this dialogue might sound somewhat familiar to you.

PAGE 7, PANEL 4: "On Mount Olympus, the home of the gods. The tallest mountain left standing after their war with the Titans."—If you're a regular reader of these books and their attendant Greek Notes, you doubtless know that I have included this line, or some variation of it, in every volume of OLYMPIANS—*or so I thought*. Recently, an astute young reader of OLYMPIANS pointed out to me that I, in fact, do not have this line anywhere in OLYMPIANS Book 3, *Hera: The Goddess and Her Glory*. To that I say, well, nothing is perfect.

But seriously, if any reader out there has a time machine, please hit me up. I have a change I need to make.

PAGE 8, PANEL 2: You can tell this takes place early on in Olympian history, because Poseidon ain't rocking his stylish mustache yet.

PAGE 8, PANEL 4: Zeus was...elsewhere with Leto, mother of Apollo and Artemis, as we saw in OLYMPIANS Book 9, *Artemis: Wild Goddess of the Hunt*.

PAGE 9, PANELS 4–7: In some myths, Hera conceives Hephaistos alone, with no input from Zeus. Her striking the ground here, with enough force to rock Olympus, is a nod to other traditions wherein Hera conceives the monstrous Typhon solo (seen in OLYMPIANS Book 10, *Hermes: Tales of the Trickster*) by striking the earth with her palm.

PAGE 10, PANEL 1: One of the great challenges of adulthood is when your friend presents you with their ugly newborn child and you need to pretend how cute said child is. Hera would fail that test big-time.

PAGE 12, PANEL 4: We've previously met Thetis in OLYMPIANS Books 6 and 7, *Aphrodite: Goddess of Love* and *Ares: Bringer of War*. Eurynome is mentioned briefly in *Hera: The Goddess and Her Glory* and glimpsed (but not named explicitly!) in *Zeus: King of the Gods*.

PAGE 15: This is why, on page 7, Prometheus mentions that Olympus "looked different then." Whenever I draw a pre-Hephaistos Mount Olympus, I draw it in the architectural style of the Minoans, to reflect the earlier time period. Go back and check out previous installments of OLYMPIANS if you don't believe me. I tell you this now because I want you to notice how very clever I am.

PAGE 16, PANEL 3: I modeled Hephaistos's automatons on the ancient Greek Korai sculptures, with their archaic smiles. As an aside, how cool is it that Hephaistos has robots? Talk about being ahead of the curve!

PAGE 17, PANEL 2: Behold Talos, proud holder of the title of Greatest Disparity between Amount of Design Prep vs. Actual Appearance in a Book. You see, in some myths, Talos is a robot man; in others, a robot bull. As a child of the 1980s, I thought, *Ooh, I'll make him a Transformer!* I've drawn Talos about eleventy jillion times, working out both humanoid and tauroid forms and how he would transition between each—all for this one glorious panel. Bon appétit!

PAGE 20: The whole practice of burning sacrifices to the gods was initiated by Hermes in *Hermes: Tales of the*

Trickster. There was a lot of debate, back in the day, on whether or not Zeus is tricked by Prometheus here. After all, Zeus is meant to be infallible—how could he be tricked? Many of the ancient Greek writers maintained that Zeus does this on purpose, for reasons only he can discern. I leave it up to you, the reader, to decide.

PAGE 23, PANEL 6: "Strength and force" is a nod to *Prometheus Bound*, in which Hephaistos is accompanied by two entities named Kratos and Bia, whose names mean, literally, "strength" and "force."

PAGE 24, PANEL 4: You may think you have a crummy job, but imagine poor Hebe, stuck for eternity as the waitress to the gods, most of whom are her brothers and sisters.

PAGE 25, PANEL 1: "Like an Erinys"—We met the Erinyes, also known as the Furies, in OLYMPIANS Book 4, *Hades: Lord of the Dead*. Once the Erinyes have been set on a target, they will never, ever stop pursuing them. Normally, they appear in threes, but Erinys is the singular form.

PAGE 26, PANEL 6: I just want to point out how amused I am with myself for working the name Hephty-Wefty into this book.

PAGE 27, PANEL 5: I didn't invent the idea of Hephaistos harboring a crush on Athena. In fact, the legendary early ruler of Athens, Erichthonius, was born out of an aborted attempt at a union between the two gods by Hephaistos.

PAGE 28, PANEL 1: Seriously, Apollo.

PAGE 28, PANEL 3: Dionysos doesn't just bring his own drinks; he usually can be counted on to bring his own party.

PAGE 29: Santa Claus has nothing on Helios when it comes to the whole "He knows when you've been naughty" shtick.

PAGE 30, PANEL 2: The composition of this panel is an homage to the painting *Apollo in the Forge of Vulcan*, by Diego Velázquez. As an aside, if my hypothetical reader who owns a time machine could go back and let the esteemed Sr. Velázquez know that the title should be *Sol (or Helios) in the Forge of Vulcan*, I'd be much obliged, thank you.

PAGE 36, PANEL 4: Both Hermes and Prometheus could be considered trickster gods, so it makes sense that Hermes would recognize Prometheus as trouble.

PAGE 38, PANEL 1: Busts of Eurynome and Thetis, his two "moms," flank the entranceway to Hephaistos's palace.

PAGE 41, PANEL 2: Aphrodite's sandal comment here is a reference to a myth in which Hermes does eventually seduce Aphrodite by stealing her sandal. It's from that union that their child, Hermaphrodite, is born.

PAGE 42, PANEL 1: I just want to say that this is my favorite drawing of Apollo I've ever done.

PAGE 42, PANEL 7: I would love to write a three-hundred-page graphic novel of just Hermes and Apollo hanging out and being goofballs together.

PAGE 42, PANEL 9: One of my favorite cool factoids I like to throw out at parties is that at the time *The Iliad* is set, Hephaistos and Aphrodite are officially divorced! Who knew they had divorce in ancient Greece? As a sidenote, I don't get invited to many parties, and this may be why.

PAGE 43, PANEL 6: Hmmm...

PAGE 44, PANEL 3: Double hmmm...

PAGE 48, PANELS 1–4: The nature of hope being imprisoned in Pandora's jar is a great conversation starter at parties. Again, I don't get invited to many.

PAGE 48, PANEL 6: Eye see what you did there...

PAGE 50, PANEL 4: It's only in reading this now that I realize this may be an unconscious reference to the last line of the final episode of the late, lamented space-western TV show *Firefly*. Man, I like *Firefly*...

PAGE 56, PANEL 5: Gods have golden ichor flowing through their veins instead of plain ol' red blood.

PAGE 57, PANEL 4: You may have noticed that the adamantine bands holding Hera's legs seem to have disappeared. "Oho!" you undoubtedly say aloud to yourself. "I seem to have caught the illustrious Mr. O'Connor making quite the gaffe!" To which I might reply, "Not so fast, True Believer! The electricity coursing through Hera's body is glowing so brightly, it creates the illusion that the bands are transparent!" Now aren't you glad you realized I didn't make a drawing mistake? On to the next note!

PAGE 58, PANEL 3: Cue humorous trombone sound. *Womp womp wooommpp...*

PAGE 59, PANEL 1: Cue humorous trombone sound. *Ouch.*

PAGE 60, PANEL 4: Ares, master of the understatement.

PAGE 61, PANEL 6: After eleven volumes of largely hanging out in the background, Dionysos finally steps up to the plate.

PAGE 63, PANEL 5: Look for this story in the upcoming OLYMPIANS Book 12, *Dionysos: The Yet to Be Subtitled.*

PAGE 64, PANEL 2: See? I told you Dionysos brings his own party.

PAGE 66: Things end happily enough in this book for Hephaistos, but what about poor Prometheus? Well, that eagle we see in panel 6? It's flying over to Prometheus to eat his liver. Prometheus, being immortal, won't die from this, and his liver will regenerate. Unfortunately, the eagle will return EVERY DAY to eat his liver once again.

This is one of the most famous punishments in all of mythology—heck, in all of everything, period. Why is Prometheus being thusly punished? Is it for returning fire to humankind? If Zeus is so upset about that, why doesn't he just have Hephaistos take it away again?

In this book, Hermes insinuates that the real reason Prometheus is being punished is that his power of prophecy has revealed to him Zeus's downfall. That's not my invention—that is pretty explicitly the reason he is being bound in *Prometheus Bound*. That play ends with Prometheus refusing to tell Hermes what he knows (or claims to know) and Zeus sending Prometheus to Tartarus with a lightning bolt, to be continued in part two of the Promethean trilogy, *Prometheus Unbound*.

Only problem is, *Prometheus Unbound* has essentially been lost to us. Just a few lines remain. Even less remains of what we think was the third part, *Prometheus the Fire-Bringer*. We're left never really knowing what Prometheus knows, or doesn't know, about the downfall of Zeus. Many people think that eventually, it was revealed that the downfall Prometheus sees is Zeus having a child with Thetis, a child destined to be greater than his father—a fate we saw averted in OLYMPIANS Book 6, *Aphrodite: Goddess of Love*. But without the missing parts of the story, well, we'll never know for sure what is revealed to Prometheus.

Don't worry about Prometheus, though. One thing he does know is what's coming for him. Much like Zeus's rule, this punishment isn't going to be eternal. After thirteen generations of torment, he'll be freed by Heracles. Piece of cake.

HELIOS

HE WHO RISES ABOVE

TITAN OF He is literally the Sun.

ROMAN NAME Sol

SYMBOLS The Sun, his Chariot

SACRED ANIMALS Horse, Rooster (the animal that announces his arrival every day)

SACRED PLANT The Heliotrope (a flower that turns its face to follow the Sun across the sky)

SACRED PLACE The island of Rhodes (site of the Colossus of Rhodes, an, uh, colossal statue of Helios and one of the seven wonders of the ancient world)

HEAVENLY BODY Just a little star we like to call the SUN

MODERN LEGACIES The element helium is named after this Titan because it was first detected in our atmosphere during a solar eclipse, in 1868.

Speaking of solar, the word "solar," as in solar system, is derived from the Roman name for this Titan.

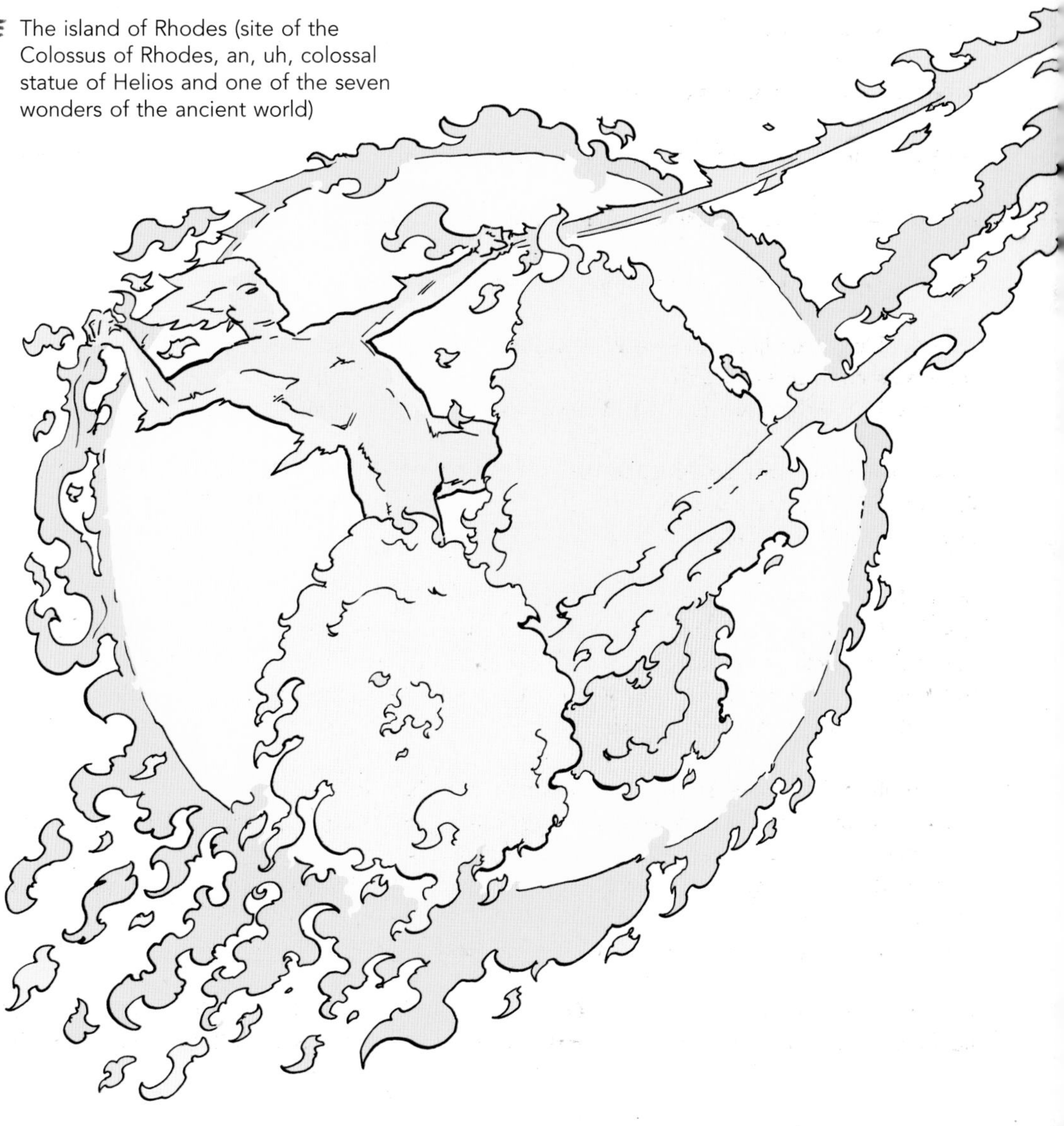

PROMETHEUS

THE FIRE-BRINGER

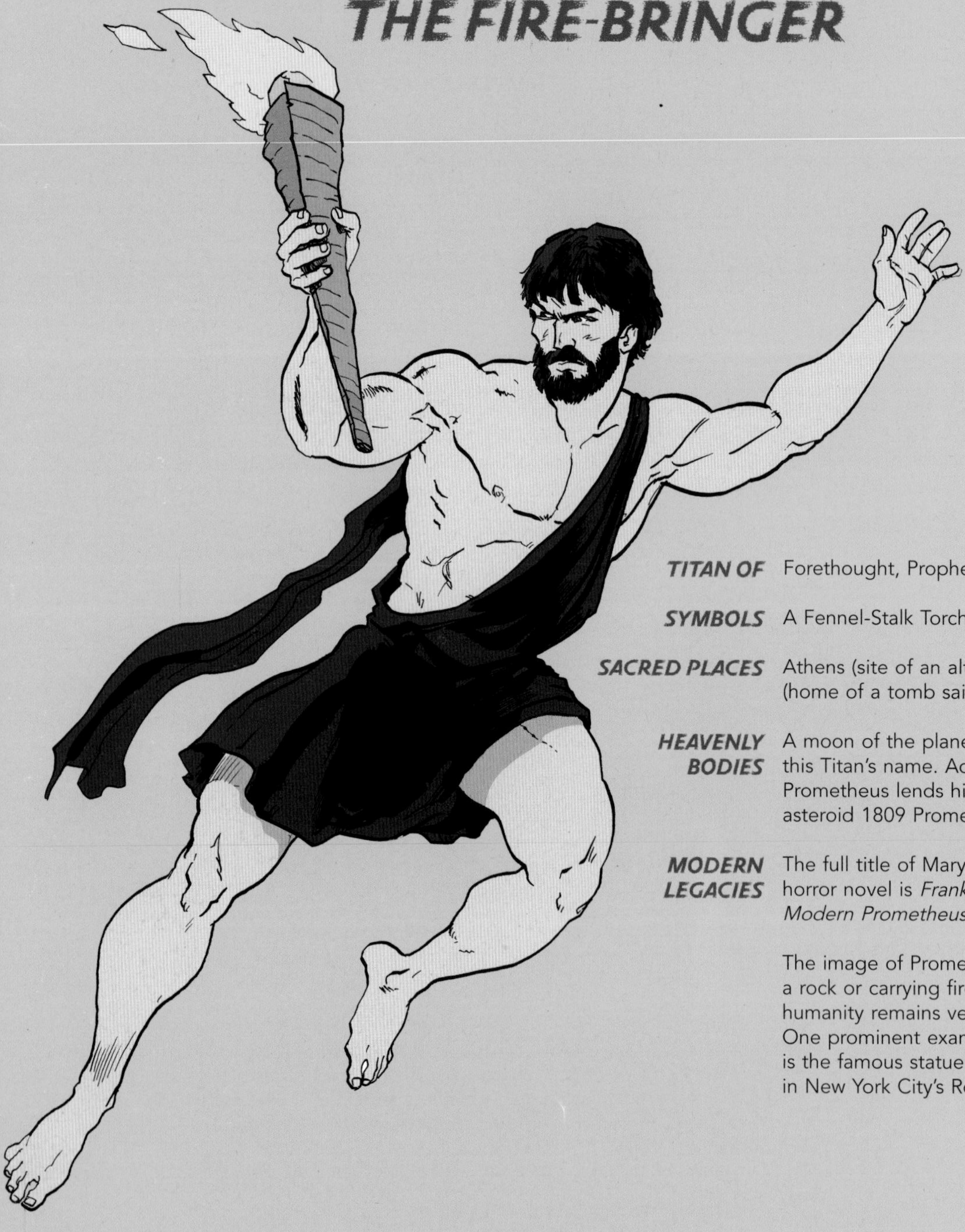

TITAN OF Forethought, Prophecy

SYMBOLS A Fennel-Stalk Torch, Fire

SACRED PLACES Athens (site of an altar to him), Argos (home of a tomb said to be his)

HEAVENLY BODIES A moon of the planet Saturn bears this Titan's name. Additionally, Prometheus lends his name to the asteroid 1809 Prometheus.

MODERN LEGACIES The full title of Mary Shelley's famous horror novel is *Frankenstein: or, the Modern Prometheus*, after this Titan.

The image of Prometheus chained to a rock or carrying fire back down to humanity remains very well known. One prominent example of the latter is the famous statue by Paul Manship in New York City's Rockefeller Center.

ABOUT THIS BOOK

HEPHAISTOS: GOD OF FIRE is the eleventh book in OLYMPIANS, a graphic novel series from First Second that retells the Greek myths.

FOR DISCUSSION

1 Who is more wrong to throw Hephaistos off Olympus, Zeus or Hera? Who deserves more to be stuck to that chair?

2 This book is all about punishments. Prometheus is bound, Ares and Aphrodite chained, Hera stuck to her throne. Are these appropriate punishments? Who else might deserve to be punished?

3 Why do you think hope is left in Pandora's jar?

4 Which of Hephaistos's inventions do you think is the best? What other things might Hephaistos have invented?

5 Do you think Zeus is tricked at Mekone, or does he just pretend to be?

6 Why do you think Zeus has Prometheus shackled? What do you think Prometheus knows?

7 The Olympians are, at heart, shape-shifters. We know Hephaistos can take other forms—so why do you suppose he appears as an ugly man? For that matter, why doesn't he heal his impaired legs?

8 Very few people believe in the Greek gods today. Why do you think it's important that we still learn about them?

BIBLIOGRAPHY

PROMETHEUS BOUND.
AESCHYLUS, NEW YORK: OXFORD UNIVERSITY PRESS, 1990.
There are many editions of this play out there, but I used the one translated by James Scully and C. John Herington. What I like about this version is that it also contains the surviving fragments of the rest of the Prometheus trilogy.

THE ILIAD OF HOMER.
TRANSLATED BY RICHMOND LATTIMORE. CHICAGO: UNIVERSITY OF CHICAGO PRESS, 1951.
The account of Hephaistos's childhood on Lemnos came from here, as well as his being thrown off Olympus by Zeus. Additionally, the sequence of Hephaistos serving drinks on Olympus was largely repurposed from a scene in *The Iliad*. Much like *Prometheus Bound*, there are many translations of *The Iliad* available, but I used this particular version as it's widely held that Lattimore does the best job of preserving the flavor of the ancient Greek.

THE ODYSSEY OF HOMER.
TRANSLATED BY RICHMOND LATTIMORE. NEW YORK: HARPER PERENNIAL, 1991.
Wow, a lot of Homer in this book! Way to go, Homer! He normally ends up taking a back seat to Hesiod, but I really prefer the Homeric Hephaistos. Pretty much the entire sequence of the invisible chaining of Aphrodite and Ares came from here.

HESIOD: VOLUME 1, THEOGONY.
WORKS AND DAYS: TESTIMONIA. HESIOD, NEW YORK: LOEB CLASSICAL LIBRARY, 2007.
I don't particularly like a lot of what Hesiod writes about Hephaistos (a big feh! from me on his being born from Hera alone), but I did pull a fair amount from his account of the creation of Pandora.

AESOP'S FABLES.
TRANSLATED BY LAURA GIBBS. NEW YORK: OXFORD UNIVERSITY PRESS, 2002.
I read quite a bit of fables back when I was writing *Hermes: Tales of the Trickster*, and discovered that a few of them mention Pandora's jar—and, specifically, debate about the nature of that entombed hope—so I figured I'd give it a nod here.

THEOI GREEK MYTHOLOGY WEB SITE WWW.THEOI.COM
Without a doubt, the single most valuable resource I came across in this entire venture. At Theoi.com, you can find an encyclopedia of various gods and goddesses from Greek mythology, cross-referenced with every mention of them they could find in literally hundreds of ancient Greek and Roman texts. Unfortunately, it's not quite complete, and it doesn't seem to be updated anymore.

WWW.LIBRARY.THEOI.COM
A subsection of the above site, it's an online archive of hundreds of ancient Greek and Roman texts. Many of these have never been published in the traditional sense, and many are just fragments recovered from ancient papyrus, or recovered text from other authors' quotations of lost epics. Invaluable.

ALSO RECOMMENDED
FOR YOUNGER READERS

D'Aulaires' Book of Greek Myths. Ingri and Edgar Parin D'Aulaire. New York: Doubleday, 1962.

FOR OLDER READERS

The Marriage of Cadmus and Harmony. Robert Calasso. New York: Knopf, 1993.

Mythology. Edith Hamilton. New York: Grand Central Publishing, 1999.

PANDORA

THE ONE WITH ALL THE GIFTS

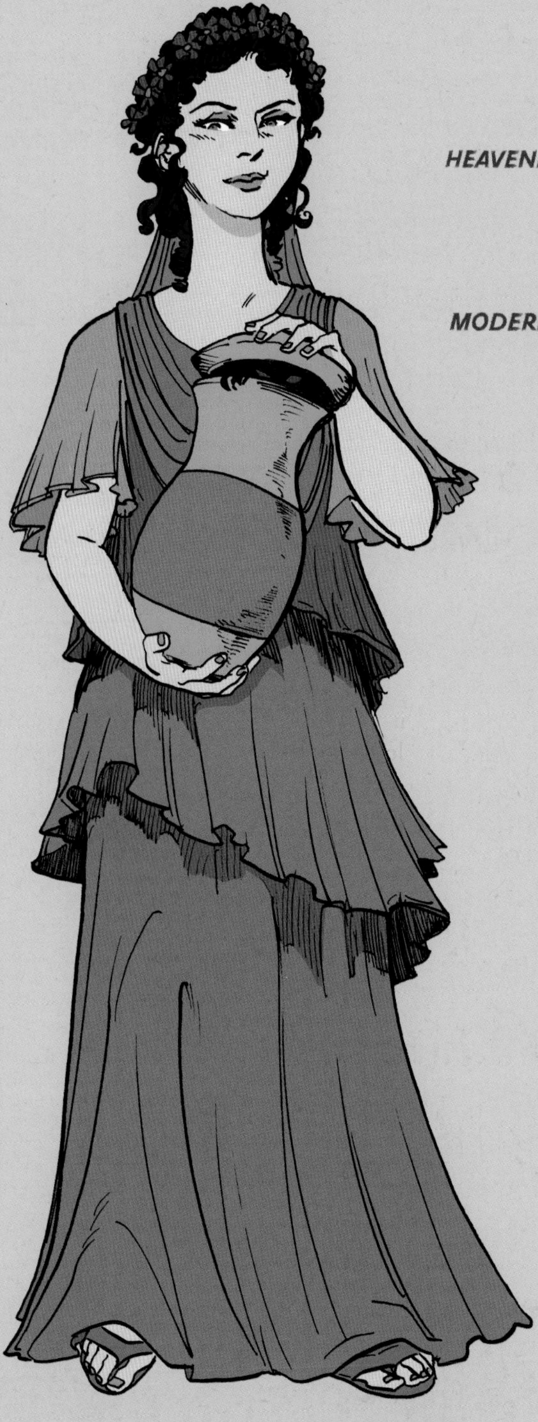

SYMBOL A Pithos (jar)

HEAVENLY BODIES Two—an asteroid, 55 Pandora, and a moon of the planet Saturn. Pandora is also the name of the fictional moon that serves as the setting for James Cameron's *Avatar*.

MODERN LEGACY The popular music streaming service Pandora takes its name from this figure.

The term "Pandora's box" has come to mean any action or situation that results in a great deal of unexpected trouble. An example of this idiom in use may be "Boy, I sure opened a Pandora's box when I decided to write all this back matter when I started this series."

For Nicole

—G. O.

First Second

New York

Copyright © 2019 by George O'Connor

Published by First Second
First Second is an imprint of Roaring Brook Press,
a division of Holtzbrinck Publishing Holdings Limited Partnership
175 Fifth Avenue, New York, NY 10010

Don't miss your next favorite book from First Second! Sign up for our enewsletter to get
updates at firstsecondnewsletter.com.

Library of Congress Control Number: 2018938079

Paperback ISBN: 978-1-62672-528-7
Hardcover ISBN: 978-1-62672-527-0

Our books may be purchased in bulk for promotional, educational, or business use. Please contact your local
bookseller or the Macmillan Corporate and Premium Sales Department at
(800) 221-7945 ext. 5442 or by e-mail at MacmillanSpecialMarkets@macmillan.com.

FIRST
EDITION

First edition, 2019

Book design by Rob Steen

Printed in China by Toppan Leefung Printing Ltd., Dongguan City, Guangdong Province

Paperback: 10 9 8 7 6 5 4 3 2 1
Hardcover: 10 9 8 7 6 5 4 3 2 1